MW01126664

Decisions

and

Consequences

By Zoe Burton

Decisions and

Consequences

Zoe Burton

Published by Zoe Burton

Early drafts of this book were written and posted on fan fiction forums in December 2015.

Story edits completed by Serena Agusto-Cox

ISBN-10: 152346433X

ISBN-13: 978-1523464333

Acknowledgements

As always, I must first thank Jesus Christ, my Savior and Guide. Without You none of my stories would have been told. I love you!

Additional thanks go to my support system, my sisters-in-heart, Rose and Leenie. You continue to stretch me and keep me on the straight and narrow, writing-wise. You rock!!

I can't go without thanking Gail, who kept me well-supplied with killer brownies and visual inspiration while I wrote, then cold-read for me when I was finished. I wish you did not live on the other side of the country from me. If we lived close enough, I'd be camped out in your living room. ;)

Table of Contents

Prologue

Fitzwilliam Darcy stood with his friend and the man's family at the entrance to the Meryton Assembly Room, wishing he were anywhere else. He had no desire to dance, not even with Bingley's sisters. Thinking of them made him think of his own sister and the heartache she had suffered this past summer. To be taken in by a cad at such a tender age as five and ten was difficult for anyone, but for the shy and sensitive Georgiana, it was pure misery. He had spent the last two months trying to raise her spirits, reassuring her of his love and devotion. He had been rewarded with the cessation of tears on her part, though it was obvious that she was still sad. She plainly told him that her trust in herself and her judgment, not to mention men, was shaken to its core. Her new, carefully scrutinized, companion, Mrs Annesley, assured him that with time, Georgiana would recover. He could only trust that she was correct.

Fitzwilliam had felt the pain right along with his young sister. He was no stranger to being lied to; led to believe one thing while something quite different was the actual truth. He had been master of his estate for five years now, having inherited it upon his father's death a week after his two and twentieth birthday, though he had been doing the majority of the decision-making for even longer. George Darcy's demise had been expected, as he had been ill for several months prior, and it was a relief that his suffering was over. However much solace he felt that his parent was no longer in pain, a greater distress was soon to overtake him.

He had always, as the heir to Pemberley, been desirable husband material. Many a debutante's parent had thrown their daughters in his path at one soiree or another since his levee. Once his period of mourning ended and he began attending events again, it had gotten much worse. Now the debutantes were throwing *themselves* at him. Not to mention the widows looking for a new, young husband. He, however, was impervious to them. It was not that he did not feel a physical attraction, even desire, for some of them. It was difficult for a healthy young man not to respond to a woman whose attributes were as prominently displayed as most of them were, and he was most certainly healthy. For Fitzwilliam, the fact of the matter was that not only did he take attendance at church and adherence to its precepts to heart; he also had definite ideas about his future wife. He had a list,

Decisions and Consequences

tucked into his journal, of the attributes he considered essential. At
the top of the list was honesty.

Fitzwilliam had loved both of
his parents. He had been very close
to his mother until her death when
he was six and ten and Georgiana
was four. He had grieved deeply for
her. His love for his father was
slightly different. His father had a
love borne more of respect than a
parental bond. His mother had encouraged him to feel and discuss his
emotions in a safe manner. His father trained him to run the estate,
and that training began at an early
age. There was little room for emotion in his methods.

From the time Fitzwilliam was
old enough to sit up, his father had
taken him along while he surveyed
Pemberley. Short trips at first, of
course, that got longer after each
birthday. When he was old enough
for his own pony, he stopped riding
in front of his father and began to

10

learn to ride alongside. And while they rode, father taught son little bits of estate management here and there, so that by the time George Darcy passed away, Fitzwilliam was running the family properties with skill and decisiveness. This education and its methods were what earned the man his son's respect.

However, Fitzwilliam knew that neither of his parents was perfect. He knew that his father had kept a mistress in London, even while his wife was alive, and he further knew that his mother was aware. He was witness to her tears on more than one occasion as his father rode off to town. He also knew that his mother was not above manipulating his father to get what she wanted. He had been a quiet and observant child and had seen much of which his parents were unaware.

As he grew, he decided that he did not want to live as his parents had. Both frequently spoke to him of duty to family. He knew what was expected of him as a Darcy and as a member of the *ton*. He also knew that he needed to marry someone who shared his values. What he would do if he could not find a wife amongst the members of his circle, he did not know. Perhaps he would never marry and Georgiana's son would inherit.

Still, after three or four years of running Pemberley and raising his sister alone, Fitzwilliam decided to begin searching for a wife in earnest. He attended more of the despised balls and dinners than he had in the past, and actually asked young ladies to dance. He forced himself to make small talk with them, and evaluated each based on his list. What he found was a disappointment.

Every woman he danced with agreed with every word he said. No matter that he changed his position on a subject five or six times within one conversation, they always agreed. Few were able to discuss serious works of literature or current events. They fawned over him, as well, and he hated it. The worst of them all was Lady Sarah Stanton.

He had called upon her more often than any other, and had thought that she might be the one he chose. She was charming, witty, and well-read. She was beautiful in the classic sense, tall and willowy. She did not inspire his baser nature, but he thought that he certainly would not mind bedding her. She had appeared to be honest in her opinions, as well. Fitzwilliam had no more made the decision to officially court her than he overheard her at a ball, on the terrace, telling another man that she thought he was arrogant and boring and that she was only hoping for a proposal from him for his money. She had gone on to tell the man that marriage to Fitzwilliam would not interfere with her affair with him.

Decisions and Consequences

His hurt and anger at what he saw as a betrayal were severe. He was furious! He made his presence known to her and her companion immediately, informing her in a low voice that their acquaintance was severed and that she would be turned away from his homes, should she venture there. He had then turned on his heel and strode from the terrace, fists and jaw clenched tightly. He found his hosts and made his excuses, then returned to Darcy House to find relief in pacing the floor of his chambers and cursing dishonest people of all kinds. He would have liked a more physical relief, such as fencing, but that was not to be had in the middle of the night.

Not long after this incident, just a few short weeks after, had come the one with Georgiana. The two combined had made him decide to put his search for a wife on hold. He had not attended an event since that disastrous ball, yet here he was in a small town in Hertfordshire attending an assembly full of strangers who were no doubt just as ready to lie to and about him as those in Town. How he hated being on display!

Chapter 1

As Darcy and his party stood in the doorway of the Meryton Assembly Room, he scanned the large group already gathered.

There were probably one hundred people crowded together, most around the edges of the room. There were two lines of dancers in the middle, men on one side and women on the other. The heat of so many people made a fire unnecessary, but there was a small one in the fireplace near the door, anyway. Six chandeliers dripped the wax of dozens of candles onto the revelers while at the same time adding to the room temperature. Wall sconces reflected additional candle light into the room. Darcy was not impressed with the place. It was far less elegant than what he was used to in the best houses, and at Almack's. He turned his examination from the room itself to the people gathered in it.

He was not any more inspired by them than he was by the room Their clothing was less than fashionable, and from what he could see, there was a decided lack of decorum in general, with much loud laughter and overly exuberant motions amongst the dancers. Certainly no one of his circles, the very first circles of society, would behave in such an ebullient manner. All of a sudden, the music stopped. The dancers all turned to see what had happened to cause the cessation. Silence fell over the room as every eye turned to the entrance. The center of the ballroom floor suddenly opened up to Darcy and his friends as Sir William Lucas greeted them and led them into the midst of the crowd.

Darcy's eyes moved from person to person as he walked at the back of the party. His gaze was suddenly arrested by a striking young woman standing with a small group of others. The lady had been turned away from him and toward her companion, but as she looked in his direction, a bright smile graced her face. Her brown eyes twinkled, adding an air of joy to her countenance. For a brief moment, their eyes locked and an awareness of her struck him before his attention was reclaimed by Sir William Lucas.

As his group moved further into the Assembly Hall, murmurs began to reach his ears. It was apparent that people were discussing his and Bingley's incomes. He braced himself for the mothers and daughters who would soon throw themselves at him. He hated it, but it happened everywhere he went.

Sure enough, Sir William was introducing the party to a family named Bennet. The gleam in the mother's eye as she simpered and pushed her daughters at them was unmistakable. Bingley asked the eldest, Jane he thought she was called, to stand up with him for the next. Being in no mood to dance, Darcy remained at the back of the group and quiet. He was startled when Mrs. Bennet asked him if he also liked to dance, then annoyed when she insisted, upon his denial, that he could not possibly dislike the activity. At that point, he bowed and walked away.

He was unconcerned with what the lady considered his rudeness. Darcy was of the first circles of society, and a very moral and upright man. It mattered not what a country squire's wife thought of his actions. In fact, the entire room was filled with inconsequential people. Certainly, he did not set out to be rude, but Mrs. Bennet had offended him. Nor did he care what the rest of the attendees thought of him. He would leave here at the end of his visit with Bingley and never see them again.

~~~***~~~

While his friend was pacing the edges of the room with a dark scowl on his face, Bingley was enjoying a dance with the most beautiful creature he had ever beheld. He could see Darcy making a circuit around the edge of the dance floor and looking thunderous. He determined to coax him to participate just as soon as his dance with the lovely Miss Bennet was complete.

After returning his partner to her mother's side, Bingley scanned the room, finally locating Darcy standing alone. Striding quickly, he approached his friend and began speaking.

"Darcy, I must have you dance! I hate to see you standing about in this stupid manner!" Bingley then gestured to Elizabeth, having seen her sitting behind his friend, offering to have his dance partner, the beautiful Miss Jane Bennet, introduce them. Darcy looked over his shoulder and made eye contact with her, then turned his glare back to his friend and said, "She is tolerable, I suppose, but not handsome enough to tempt me, and I am in no humor at present to give consequence to young ladies who are slighted by other men. You had better return to your partner and enjoy her smiles, for you are wasting your time with me."

Bingley shook his head at his oldest friend. Surely Darcy was aware that the young lady was close enough to hear him speak! Sometimes the man's arrogance was beyond belief.

~~~***~~~

As Bingley moved away, back towards Miss Bennet, Darcy became aware of voices behind him. They were quiet voices, but he was close enough to clearly hear them. He heard his name; Miss Bennet's sister must be telling someone what he had said of her. He stiffened as she shared with someone, another female judging by the giggles he heard, what he had said. Soon the voices seemed a bit more clear.

"I would not dance with him if he asked. Such an arrogant and conceited man can have no interest to me. He can have his ten thousand a year and half of Derbyshire. He is not worthy to wipe my boots."

By this time, Darcy was standing rigidly, containing his affront with a set face and stiff, straight muscles. He turned his head to catch sight of the back of the lady's green-trimmed ivory gown as she marched stiffly away. Just who did she think she was? A country Miss with no refinement and no worth. *I bet she has no connections worth knowing, either,* he thought.

Decisions and Consequences

Darcy spent the rest of the evening as he had begun it, though he did dance once with each of Bingley's sisters. He began to find, though, that his eyes kept returning to the lady he had rejected, who had insulted him in her turn. She enjoyed dancing, if the smile on her face and the laugh on her lips were any indication. She was required to sit out a few sets, as there did not appear to be an adequate number of gentlemen in attendance. His conscience bit him some about that. He was not sure his parents would have liked his refusal to dance when there were so few gentlemen available. To dance in such a situation would have been considered doing his duty in their minds, he was sure.

As he watched the Bennet girl, he was struck by her manners. She was friendly to all, and polite. He began to notice a difference, though, in how she behaved with some people as compared to others. To her sister and friend she was warm, smiling invitingly and teasing. There were others to whom she was polite and correct but no more, still with a smile, but without that extra bit of warmth that characterized her interactions with those to whom she was close. There was no falseness in her interactions with those around her. If one took the trouble to watch, one would see that though she was polite and friendly to all, she was only warm and teasing with those closest to her. Darcy found that he liked that aspect of her personality, though he could not say that he liked her as a person. As the evening drew to a close, he pushed the young lady and her pertness to the back of his mind, relieved to be returning to Netherfield.

~~~***~~~

Elizabeth Bennet and her sister, Kitty, spun away from each other at the end of a set of dances at

Decisions and Consequences

the Meryton Assembly, laughing. They were standing up together due to a lack of gentlemen in attendance, but both enjoyed dancing too much to mind with whom they were partnered. After curtseying to each other and laughing, they each headed in a different direction—Kitty to find their youngest sister, Lydia, and Elizabeth to collect a cup of punch from the refreshment area.

Upon receiving her cup and bestowing a thankful smile on the servant who was tending the table, she wound her way through the crowded assembly room until she came to her dearest sister, Jane, and her oldest friend, Charlotte Lucas. Jane Bennet was older than Elizabeth by two years and was by far the prettiest of the five daughters of Thomas and Fanny Bennet. The two sisters were very close, and one was rarely seen at a public function without the other being in close proximity.

"Oh, Jane, Charlotte, was that not the liveliest dance you have ever seen?"

"Indeed, Lizzy, it was," Jane smiled at her next youngest sister. "You and Kitty appeared to be having a wonderful time of it."

"We were! How grateful I was that she agreed to stand up with me; otherwise I would have missed a very entertaining set, and you know that I love to laugh."

Charlotte, a smile on her face and a giggle on her lips, interjected with, "Oh yes, Elizabeth. We know you do!"

The trio's attention was drawn to the entrance of the room by a sudden commotion. There the girls saw a group of five standing in front of the doors, three gentlemen and two ladies. Charlotte's father, Sir William Lucas, was bowing to the group and welcoming them to the humble Assembly. Sir William had been in trade and had once been

27

mayor of Meryton, the small town in Hertfordshire in which the assembly hall was located and where most of the gathered attendees lived.

"This must be the famous Bingley party," Elizabeth whispered to her friend, turning towards Charlotte and leaning close.

"It is," affirmed her friend, going on to explain who each member of the group was. Charlotte had gained this intelligence from her father, who had been one of many men in the area to call on Mr. Bingley to welcome him to the neighborhood.

"Well," Jane stated, "at least there are not as many ladies as was rumored to be."

"True, Sister. Let us hope they are inclined to dance!" The friends shared another laugh then turned to watch as Sir William led the newcomers around the room to begin introductions. Examining the group, Elizabeth's eye was drawn to one of them. She found that she could not look away from the tall, dark-haired man keeping to the back of the bunch. He was the most handsome gentleman she had ever seen. He was tall with straight dark hair that just brushed his collar. His clothing, she could see even from this distance, was well-tailored, fitting closely to his broad shoulders and trim waist. He looked up and her gaze was caught in his intense, startlingly-blue-eyed one for a brief few seconds, until she colored and forced herself to look away. She realized her heart was pounding in her chest; she could not account for it. *It must be embarrassment,* she reasoned, *at being caught staring.* It could not possibly have anything to do with the interest she had seen in his eyes.

Mrs. Bennet soon rushed up to the group of young ladies, grasping her eldest by the hand and almost dragging her to the spot where Mr. Bennet stood. The mother of five daughters with little dowry wanted to make sure that her most beautiful daughter was introduced as soon as possible to the newly arrived gentlemen. She lived in fear of being thrown into the hedgerows to starve upon her husband's death and was quite eager to marry her girls off to any man that would have them. Jane, though.....Jane she expected to make a spectacular match. She could not be so beautiful for nothing, you know.

The mother and her daughters had no more than arrived at Mr. Bennet's side than Sir William, along with Mr. Bingley and his friends, were before them and introductions commenced. Elizabeth cast a few surreptitious looks at the friend, who was introduced as Mr. Darcy of Pemberley and Derbyshire. Mr. Bingley asked Jane to dance, as expected, but Mr. Darcy walked away without asking anyone for a set.

Elizabeth was not sure what to think of this unusual and unsociable behavior. She was certainly disappointed. She loved to dance and to socialize, and she would have enjoyed getting to know the man a little better. However, the confusion and cordial feelings she was harboring toward him changed later in the evening, after hearing Mr. Darcy insult her.

Elizabeth sat in shock at what she had heard. Her initial response was hurt. She knew she had no astonishing beauty. That was Jane's forte. Still, to be dismissed in such a manner and in such a place! Who knew which of their neighbors had overheard? Her second response, which came quickly upon the first, was anger. How dare he humiliate her! He knew nothing of her! All curiosity about the man died in her breast. She had no desire to know better a man who was so rude and censorious. Indeed, she would not dance with him now if he were to ask. She would rather sit out the remainder of the evening than to stand up with such a pompous and arrogant man.

As infuriated as she was, Elizabeth was not able to sit quietly any longer. Spying Charlotte standing nearby, she rose from her seat and went to stand beside her.

"Lizzy, what is the matter?" Charlotte could see that her friend was disturbed. She listened with amazement as Elizabeth related what she had heard. A quick glance in Mr. Darcy's direction told her that, though his back was to them, he likely could hear them, so she nudged her friend and nodded in his direction.

Seeing the man's location and harboring a desire that he should know her displeasure, Elizabeth grabbed Charlotte's arm and moved them two steps closer before she said, "I would not dance with him if he asked. Such an arrogant and conceited man can have no interest to me. He can have his ten thousand a year and half of Derbyshire. He is not worthy to wipe my boots."

With that, she walked away, leaving her friend staring in astonishment and Mr. Darcy quietly fuming.

Chapter 2

A few days following the Assembly, Sir William Lucas entertained many of the local families in his home. He had issued the invitation primarily as a way to welcome the Bingleys and their guests to Meryton. He was a friendly and congenial man who enjoyed hosting his neighbors, entertaining them, and being entertained in return.

Sir William wandered around the room, chatting with each guest in turn and making sure they were comfortable. He soon came near to the pianoforte, where Miss Mary Bennet was playing a beautiful concerto; he paused for a moment to enjoy the sound. When Miss Mary's youngest sister, Miss Lydia, came running up and loudly requested music to dance to, he gently encouraged Miss Mary to comply, though he knew it gave her no pleasure. Before long, the two youngest Bennet daughters had officers lined up with them.

As he resumed his circuit of the room, he came to Mr. Darcy, standing alone at the edge of the area that had been cleared for the dancing. He did his best to engage the gentleman in conversation, asking him about dancing at St. James' and about his house in London. Mr. Darcy was polite, but did not encourage conversation, though Sir William was not about to let that stop him. Soon, he spotted Miss Elizabeth walking toward them and had an idea.

"Miss Elizabeth," he exclaimed, "why are you not dancing?" Turning to his neighbor, he continued, "Mr. Darcy, you must allow me to present this young lady to you as a very desirable partner. You cannot refuse to dance, I am sure, when so much beauty is before you." He took Miss Elizabeth's hand, to give it to the gentleman, but she instantly drew back.

"Indeed, Sir, I have not the least intention of dancing. Please do not think I moved this way to beg for a partner." Elizabeth was discomposed by Sir William's actions and words; she did not like Mr. Darcy and was certain he did not like her. She did not wish to dance with him, now or ever.

As surprised as he was by the proposal, Mr. Darcy was of a mind to accept, and gravely asked Miss Elizabeth to honor him with her hand, but she was steadfast in her refusal and neither his entreaties nor Sir William's attempts at persuasion would entice her to change her mind.

These actions did not injure her with Mr. Darcy, contrary to what one might think. His opinion of her was already low. He was aware of her sharp tongue and propensity to express thoughts and feelings that ought to be kept to herself. No, he did not like her. What he did like, however, was that she, in her dislike, did not attempt to curry favor with him as so many women of the *ton* were wont to do. She was honest in her disapprobation.

She had other good qualities. From what he had seen of Miss Elizabeth so far, she was attractive. Her face, while not classically pretty, was enhanced by fine eyes that sparkled when she was amused and shot fire when she was angered. Despite what he had said to Bingley, she definitely was handsome enough to tempt him, physically. And, he appreciated the honesty she displayed. She had heard his insult at the assembly, and disliked it and him and made no pretense of friendship as a result. Finally, she had pleasing manners in company, as he had observed this very evening. He compared her to the high society women he had met during his recent, unsuccessful, period of

wife-hunting, and to his list of requirements. She met a large number
of the criteria on that list. She certainly was no more or less accomplished than any other woman he
had met. She would make a fine wife
and Mistress of Pemberley, he was
convinced. He determined to observe
her more closely, to make sure of his
decision, before approaching her.

The day following the dinner
at the Lucas' saw Jane in receipt of
a note from Caroline Bingley, inviting her to dine. Jane happily requested the use of the carriage from
her father, but the horses were
needed on the farm that day and
were, therefore, unavailable. She
would have to ride. Mrs. Bennet
was quite gleeful about this; in fact,
it was her idea. It looked like rain,
and she was sure that her eldest
would be unable to return home and
the Bingleys would insist that she
stay the night. In her mind, this, of
course, meant that Jane and Mr.

Decisions and Consequences

Bingley would be able to spend more time together and she could work to secure him sooner.

Neither Elizabeth nor her father was pleased when it began to rain heavily no more than ten or fifteen minutes after she left. They were sure she would arrive soaked to the skin, and could only hope she would not become ill as a result. As her mother had predicted, Jane was forced to stay the night with the Bingleys. It was not until the next day that the full import of Mrs. Bennet's scheme was felt.

A note arrived during breakfast for Elizabeth from her sister. Jane had fallen ill from the soaking and chill she had received the day before. Elizabeth immediately determined to set off for Netherfield to nurse her sister back to health.

"I suppose this means you will want the carriage?"

"No, Papa, I am happy to walk. It is only three miles."

"Three miles in all that mud? You will not be fit to be seen! Jane will do very well with Mr. Bingley's sisters. There is nothing for you there. You had better remain here, in case the officers come to visit." Meryton had recently become the temporary home of a militia unit. Mrs. Bennet, along with Elizabeth's two youngest sisters, Kitty and Lydia, was enamored of them and saw them as potential husbands for her girls.

"Mama, I am sure that the Bingley ladies are not the sort to sit at someone's bedside for hours. I will be going to see Jane and for no other reason."

Finally able to assure her parents, Elizabeth took off across field and stile until she reached the neighboring estate. She avoided the road, sticking to cattle trails and walking paths, for the simple reason that it was quicker to travel cross-country. She jumped the puddles and mud holes as best she could, but did not allow the inconvenience of dirty shoes and hem to detract from her enjoyment of the sunshine. After the gray and cloudy sky the day before, and her mother's ridiculousness in sending Jane out in the rain, the vigorous exercise and beautiful surroundings eased her mind.

Jane was very sick indeed, though it was only a cold. Mrs. Bennet's purpose in sending her on horseback was rendered null, as Jane was sick enough to keep to her room for most of the visit. Once her fever had broken, it was only a couple of days before she was able to join the group for dinner, which was a relief to Elizabeth.

In her opinion, the only person who showed any true interest in Jane's comfort, not to mention being polite to Elizabeth herself, was Mr. Bingley. He inquired after her several times each day and was eager to provide whatever might aid in her comfort and recovery. He even sat with

Jane at her bedside twice and spent an hour or two reading aloud to her. Elizabeth made sure to seat herself in the corner and remain quiet during these times. She was happy to do what she could to further Mr. Bingley's attachment to her sister.

Mr. Darcy, unlikeable man that he was, spent his time either staring at her in disgust or arguing with her. It was all she could do to keep a civil tongue in her head! In point of fact, she did get a little sharp with him on occasion.

The first time was just two days after her arrival. She had been sitting on a settee, losing herself in a book when Miss Bingley unexpectedly requested her company on a tour about the room. Though greatly surprised at this remarkable act of civility on the part of a normally supercilious woman, Elizabeth was inclined to humor her, putting aside her book and allowing her hostess to link their arms.

Decisions and Consequences

They had made no more than one complete circuit of the large drawing room when Miss Bingley invited Mr. Darcy to join them. When he responded impertinently, saying he could admire them much better from his place by the fire, the lady responded with a patently false offense.

"How shocking! Miss Elizabeth, how shall we answer such a statement?"

"It should not be too difficult, for one such as you who is so well-acquainted with him. We can laugh at him, tease him."

"Tease him! Oh, no! We cannot tease Mr. Darcy."

Elizabeth did not think much of this, and it showed in her expression as she turned to the gentleman. "Mr. Darcy is not to be teased? Are you a man without fault, sir?"

Darcy moved uncomfortably in his chair. He, like many of his sex, did not like his weaknesses exposed. However, he would not be rude no matter how she challenged him. "I did not say I was without fault. If I have one, it is probably that I am too quick to hold a grudge. My good opinion, once lost, is lost forever."

His antagonist shook her head. "An implacable temper is definitely a shade in a character, and not one at which I can laugh. You are safe from me, Mr. Darcy. What a shame, for I dearly love to laugh!"

"I have made it a habit to avoid those situations that would make me look foolish and expose me to ridicule, Miss Bennet."

"Oh, really?" She paused a moment. "I would never laugh at what is wise and good. The follies and whims and inconsistencies of others do amuse me, however. And you, Mr. Darcy, have provided plenty of that!" She turned to the other occupants of the room, who had stopped what they were doing to watch the drama unfold. Curtseying, she said, "I must return to Jane. I will bid you all good night." She swept from the room, leaving her still-silent listeners frozen to their seats.

The worst instance occurred one evening near the end of her stay. She was standing by the pianoforte, looking at some music lying there while Miss Bingley played, when Mr. Darcy approached.

"Miss Bennet," he began, "would you not like to take this opportunity to dance a reel with me?"

Elizabeth smiled at him but returned to her perusal of the sheets before her, making no reply. Mr. Darcy was surprised at her silence, and so repeated his question.

"Oh, I heard you," Elizabeth replied. "But I do not know how to answer. I am sure you wanted me to say, 'yes', and then you would have reason to despise my taste. However, I am not about to let that happen. I do not want to dance with you, Mr. Darcy. Now despise me if you will." With that, Elizabeth walked away to sit on a nearby sofa with a book of poetry that had been sitting on the side table.

Certainly, after such a display, Mr. Darcy had to have become aware of her dislike of him. It was not as though she hid it. After this incident, Elizabeth went out of her way to avoid him, even keeping entirely to herself when the two were in the library the day before she left and refusing to speak to him.

What she did not know, however, was that her actions only made her more interesting to Mr. Darcy. By the end of the Bennet girls' visit to Netherfield, that gentleman, after watching her deflect Miss Bingley's and Mrs. Hurst's barbs with grace and aplomb, not to mention her pointed avoidance and obvious dislike of his person, was more certain than ever that he wanted this woman as Mistress of Pemberley. Never before had he seen such honesty in a woman combined with tact and grace.   Her manners were nearly flawless.   She was more playful in company than was fashionable, to be sure, but she handled difficult situations in a way that would make his aunt, Lady Matlock, proud.   In addition, he could see that she maintained a cheerful outlook even in the face of the active dislike of her hostess.   He was certain that, once they were married, she would put away her dislike of him and learn to see things in him and their marriage that were good.   *Hopefully, that happens sooner rather than later,* he thought.   *Living with a woman who actively dislikes me would be difficult.*

Now that he had made a decision, he needed to plan a strategy. He knew the Bennets' connections were negligible, and that Elizabeth's dowry was minuscule, but he did not believe financial matters would sway her to agree to marry him.   If that had been the case, she would have courted his favor despite not liking him. He could not offer her love. Indeed, he did not like her either. Truly, he had given up on the idea of love in marriage, anyway. If he had to marry for convenience, he would rather it be to someone he knew would be honest in her dealings. To this end, he decided to pay more attention to his hostess and her sister, to learn what he could of the Bennets' situation. In addition, he decided to send an express to his solicitor in Town, asking him to investigate Mr. Bennet and his connections. Mr. Darcy needed all the information he could find to help him in his quest.

Five days after Elizabeth's arrival, the two eldest Bennet girls left Netherfield for home. Elizabeth was never so glad to leave a place in her life!

~~~***~~~

Back at Longbourn, Mrs. Bennet was none too pleased that

her daughters were home two days earlier than she had planned.

"Nonsense!" She loudly proclaimed when Elizabeth stated her belief that they had been an imposition on the Bingleys. "I am quite certain Mr. Bingley was delighted to have Jane in his home."

"That may have been true, but Miss Bingley was less pleased, and she made her displeasure quite clear."

"Oh, poo! I do not believe that for a moment! You have dragged your sister out in the weather when she should have stayed at Netherfield. She shall have a relapse and never see Mr. Bingley again to secure him! Then we will be thrown to the hedgerows when your father is gone and it will all be your fault!"

Elizabeth rolled her eyes at this. *Mama, you are totally unreasonable,* she thought.

Mr. Bennet was more pleased to see his Jane and Elizabeth come home. He kissed their foreheads in welcome and expressed to them his relief that sense would finally be heard at Longbourn once again. Around mid day, when the family gathered for refreshments, Mr. Bennet shared some important information with his wife.

"I hope, Mrs. Bennet, that you have ordered a fine dinner today," her husband said to her. "We are to have a guest."

"Who is coming to visit?" his wife asked.

After glaring at his youngest two daughters, who had interrupted the discussion he was attempting to have with his spouse, the gentleman continued.

"It is someone I have never met before in all my life. My cousin, Mr. Collins, is coming for a fortnight's stay. He wrote the most amusing letter." Here, he read to his family parts of the missive. They were, in general, greatly diverted by it, except for Mrs. Bennet, who loudly expressed her displeasure.

"Do you think him a sensible man, Father?" asked his second and most intelligent daughter.

"No, Elizabeth, I do not think he is. In fact, I have great hopes of the opposite!"

Mr. Bennet was a very intelligent man, who, like his daughter, enjoyed making sport of the follies and vices of his neighbors and family. Indeed, she learned such behavior at his knee. This might not have been such a bad thing if the man was not also indolent in his dealings with his family and his estate. Longbourn had been in the family for hundreds of years and had once been very prosperous. Under Mr. Bennet, however, it had faltered. It still produced a steady two thousand pounds per annum, but that money was used as quickly as it was earned.

Neither he nor his wife had been concerned at first with economy, as they planned to have a son who would inherit the estate, which was entailed in default of heirs male. Unfortunately, by the time the fifth daughter had arrived, along with the realization that there would be no heir, the husband felt it was too late to economize, and the wife had begun using shopping as a way to make herself feel better. She had five daughters to marry off, and they must be turned out well; that was the reason she gave Mr. Bennet for her spending.

Mrs. Bennet was a beautiful woman of mean understanding and uncertain temper. As each successive daughter was born, she became less sure that she would bear an heir and more worried about her future, should something happen to cause her spouse to pass from this world. She had not a clue how the estate was run or from where the

Decisions and Consequences

funds came. As long as she had her pin money and her husband covered any overages at the shops, she was happy. When he had half-heartedly attempted, soon after Lydia's birth, to rein in her spending, she had noisily—indeed, hysterically— objected. Since then, Mr. Bennet had done as much as possible to avoid a repeat performance.

He, however, was not blameless in their lack of fortune. He enjoyed good port and good books; this is what he purchased with his portion. Both were expensive.

As a result of this lack of foresight on the part of their parents, the Bennet girls had little in the way of dowries. They would share five thousand pounds amongst themselves upon their parents' demise. It was not much to tempt a man; the Bennet girls would need to rely on their charms to make good marriages. This, of course, added to their mother's concerns.

Mr. Collins arrived exactly at the time he had mentioned in his letter. He was a tall man, and rather large, with awkward manners. He had been raised by his father, an illiterate and miserly man, as his mother had died when he was small As a result, he had a tendency towards humility. He had attended University and received ordination in the Church the previous spring, and had been grateful to be offered a valuable living as clergyman to one Lady Catherine de Bourgh of Kent. This unexpected prosperity had gone to his head, making him feel self-important. His sense of superiority, combined with the humility ingrained in him from a young age, made him ridiculous. He alternately fawned over new acquaintances and pontificated at them.

Mr. Collins was Mr. Bennet's second or third cousin, twice removed. When the elder man had been young, there was a break in the

Decisions and Consequences

family, and the Bennets and Collinses had not associated with each other for more than three decades. Upon the elder Collins' death, the younger had been reminded of his inheritance and the break between the families. As a clergyman, he thought that perhaps it might be in his best interest to heal the breach, since he was to be held more accountable by his Maker for his actions than perhaps others were. Additional incentive had come from his noble patroness, Lady Catherine, who had advised him to inspect the estate that would one day be his, and to marry a gentlewoman.

So it was that upon entering the house, Mr. Collins began effusing over the beauty of the Bennet daughters.

"I must compliment you, Mrs. Bennet, on having such a fine set of young ladies in your home! Their beauty was not at all exaggerated, as I had feared it was. I hope that you will soon find each of them well-settled in marriage."

"I thank you, sir." Mrs. Bennet, while wishing him away, was at the same time not one to turn from a compliment. "I do hope so, for with the odd way things are settled here, they will be destitute enough once Mr. Bennet has passed."

"You mean the entail, of course. I assure you, madam, that I have high hopes of making up for that unfortunate event. Well, it will be unfortunate for you, though I will then be the blessed man who becomes master. In any case, I do desire to make amends." He paused before continuing. "You are aware that I have been awarded a valuable living in Kent?"

Mrs. Bennet nodded. She was put out that he had insulted her so after complimenting her daughters.

"I have been urged by my patroness, Lady Catherine De Bourgh, to take a wife, and she suggested that

Decisions and Consequences

I choose from among your daughters. I have come prepared to admire them. Please do not fear for your future."

At this, Mrs. Bennet preened, suddenly becoming solicitous of her husband's cousin's every need.

As for Mr. Collins, he quickly decided upon the eldest as the companion of his future life. His only disquiet came when his hostess told him that his chosen daughter, Jane, was expected to be engaged any day now. Her suggestion of the second-oldest, Elizabeth, was met with enthusiasm. Yes, Miss Elizabeth was also good-looking, in her own way. She would make him a proper wife.

With this in mind, Mr. Collins began to pay Elizabeth much attention, dispensing out compliments at the same rate that he gave advice, which was often. Elizabeth was at first diverted and then annoyed with the man. It occurred to her that he might be looking to her as a future mate, but as she was not one to borrow trouble, she ignored the issue.

~~~***~~~

Two days after the arrival of their cousin, the Bennet girls decided to walk into Meryton to visit their Aunt Philips. None of them were pleased to have Mr. Collins join them, least of all Elizabeth. But as there was nothing to be done, they moved forward with their plans. Kitty and Lydia walked at the head of the group, with Elizabeth and Jane following and Mary and Mr. Collins bringing up the rear. The girls were used to this trek, as they made it several times each week, and so their steps were brisk. So great was their disgust with their cousin, however, that this day they purposely increased their stride in hopes that he would fall back. Even Mary, who at first admired him for his profession and knowledge of Scripture, was displeased with him and his fawning manner with her sister. She strode as quickly as she could to outpace him.

Mr. Collins was not in the habit of walking much. At first, his long legs allowed him to keep pace with his cousins, but soon he lagged behind. He maintained his nonstop commentary, even though he was gasping for breath. By the time he caught up with the ladies, they were at Mrs. Philips' doorstep, chatting with a soldier and another man.

"Denny! How good to see you back from London!" Lydia exclaimed.

With a bow, Lieutenant Denny replied, "Miss Lydia, it is good to see you, as well. How are you and your family?"

"Oh, we get on very well. But I missed seeing you while you were gone! I hope your business in town went well?" Lydia asked, glancing repeatedly at the handsome man standing at her friend's side.

Zoe Burton

Noticing her looks, Denny answered, "It went very well. While in town, I met with an old friend. May I introduce him to you?"

At Lydia's eager nod, he continued, "Miss Bennet, Miss Elizabeth, Miss Mary, Miss Kitty, Miss Lydia, meet Mr. Wickham. Wickham, these are the Bennet sisters."

It was at this point that Collins reached the group, and Jane introduced him to Denny and Mr. Wickham. As they finished their greetings, Collins, for once, saying little, Mr. Bingley and Mr. Darcy rode up to the group.

Elizabeth was surprised to notice Mr. Darcy and Mr. Wickham greet each other with the barest of civility. She knew the former was a generally unsociable man, but she had never before seen him be anything less than polite. She could not help but wonder at it. Before she could contemplate further, her aunt called the girls and Mr. Collins

Decisions and Consequences

inside. She did not see that Mr. Darcy gave her a long look and that Mr. Wickham noticed that look with a speculative gleam in his eye.

Chapter 3

A few days after their visit to Meryton, Mr. Bingley and his sister called on the Bennets to extend an invitation to a ball a week hence. Mrs. Bennet was sure it was in honor of Jane, and filled the house for days with her exclamations of felicity for her most beautiful daughter, regardless of the fact that said daughter was not even being courted. Her family, knowing she only saw and heard what she wanted to, saved their breath to cool their porridge and left her to it. They were well-practiced in the art of continuing a conversation as though nothing embarrassing had been said. After all, they had years to perfect the skill.

Although they had heard from their Aunt Phillips that Mr. Wickham had joined the militia and was

Decisions and Consequences

now Lieutenant Wickham, the Bennets themselves did not see him again during this time. Nor did they see any of the militia members, who were kept busy with training. Their colonel, a man named Forster, knew from previous experiences that keeping his men occupied kept them out of trouble.

It was not just maneuvers that kept the militia away. For the entirety of the four days preceding the ball, there was a steady, heavy rain. Everything needed by the five Bennet daughters for the ball that was not already purchased was gotten by proxy. To their eternal happiness, the skies cleared the morning of the ball, and the roads were dry enough to travel.

~~~***~~~

At Netherfield, preparations for the ball had proceeded apace, keeping Caroline Bingley well occupied and out of Darcy's way. For this he was grateful, for she was a model of a simpering, high society lady. He quickly tired of her fawning over him and was happy she had some employment other than seeing to his every whim.

At the moment, Darcy was in the library, out of the way of all things ball-related. He was reviewing the letter he had received the very day he had seen Wickham in Meryton. It seemed there was indeed a way to ensure acceptance of his suit with Elizabeth Bennet.

According to his solicitor, Mr. Franklin, one Thomas Bennet of Longbourn, Hertfordshire, had a very interesting history. The information Darcy held in his hand was exactly what he needed. And given Franklin's thoroughness, he was certain the information was accurate.

It seemed Mr. Bennet had defied a codicil of his father's will in marrying Mrs. Bennet. The document specified that Bennet must

Decisions and Consequences

marry a specific person, his father's
goddaughter, a lady by the name of
Miss Garnett Crofft, or in lieu of her,
another gentlewoman of the *ton,* or
forfeit his inheritance. Specifically,
he was not to marry any woman
with roots in trade.

Darcy had already learned
that Mrs. Bennet's father was a
country solicitor, and that her
brother owned and operated a very
successful import/export business.
He was, therefore, in defiance of
the terms of his father's will.
Should Darcy let word of this get
out, the Bennets would lose their
home to the heir. *That is a very
serious step to take,* he thought.
He was not entirely easy with being
the cause of a family of women losing their home. After further contemplation, he decided to hold that
as a last resort. However, having
recently learned that said heir was
currently visiting, he felt that he
should make his offer to Miss Eliz-

abeth first, and do it soon, and then speak to her father later.

He was not certain, of course, that Miss Elizabeth would accept his hand. Her dislike of him was obvious and she may be waiting for a man whom she does admire. However, Darcy knew what he wanted and was used to getting his way.

~~~***~~~

Finally, the day of the ball dawned. When the weather proved to be bright and clear, the Bennet household rejoiced, for there was nothing worse, in their collective opinion, than to find out a dance had been cancelled.

That evening, the entire family arrived in the Bennets' small carriage, with Mr. Collins in tow. As the ladies picked their way to the entrance of Netherfield while holding their skirts out of the mud, Darcy watched from a window above them.

Decisions and Consequences

He saw the stranger exit the carriage and wondered who he was and if this was the heir. When he observed the man take Miss Elizabeth's arm, it suddenly occurred to him that perhaps the heir apparent to Longbourn also had designs on the lady. He chuckled to himself as he thought of the disappointment the man was sure to feel when he realized who he was up against in the battle for the hand of Elizabeth Bennet. He turned from the window as they entered the house and made his way downstairs.

Once through the receiving line, Elizabeth and Jane made their way through to the ballroom, escorted by Mr. Bingley, who had temporarily left his sisters in charge of greeting their guests in order to settle his favorite and her sister into their places. After assuring they were well and that each had a cup of punch, Mr. Bingley went back to help Mrs. Hurst and Miss Bingley after gaining the promise of Miss Bennet's hand for the first set.

The sisters had not been sitting long when Mr. Darcy presented himself to them. After exchanging greetings, curtseys, and bows, Darcy asked Jane for a set, which she graciously gave him. Elizabeth was surprised when he then turned to her and asked, not for any available set, but for the first.

"I am sorry sir, my cousin, Mr. Collins, has asked for the first."

This was not unexpected news to Darcy, but he was still unhappy with it. However, he was not going to be deterred from his mission.

"And the second? Has that one been promised yet?"

"No, sir. I am free for the second."

"Then may I have your hand for the second set, Miss Elizabeth?"

"Yes, you may." Elizabeth handed him her dance card, watching as he scribbled his name on it. When he gave it back to her, she curtseyed to his bow and he walked away.

Turning to Jane, she exclaimed, "What was I thinking to grant him a dance?"

"You had to, Lizzy, so you did not have to sit out the rest of the evening." Jane patted her sister's hand, "All will be well. As I told you before, he watches you a great deal. I believe he admires you. And while I hope that Mr. Collins dances well, I watched Mr. Darcy at the assembly and I know for certain he is a fine dancer. Combined with the intelligence you told me he has, it is sure to be an interesting set. You will have an enjoyable time, I am sure."

"Oh, Jane. You always see the best in every situation. I wish I had a similar ability. I am certain Mr. Darcy does not admire me, and I have made plain to him my dislike of his manner."

"Ah, but I do remember you remarking on his good looks when

we talked about it after the Assembly. Is it perhaps only his behavior you dislike? He does cut a fine figure, do you not agree?" Jane sent her sister a sly glance out of the corner of her eye. One of the qualities about Jane that Elizabeth loved so much was that she had a mischievousness that only came out with those she loved the best. With most of the world, she was the model of propriety, but with her sisters, she tended to tease about slightly inappropriate things. Even having experienced this for her entire life, it always delighted Elizabeth to hear her do it.

"Jane Bennet! The things you say!" Elizabeth laughed, holding her hand over her mouth while Jane smiled widely. Controlling her laugh, if not her smile, Elizabeth continued, "Yes, Sister, he does look good, but his behavior leaves something to be desired. Even if he were interested in me in that way, and I do not believe he is, I do not know if it is enough to overcome my dislike of him."

"I am sure if you had to, you would find a way."

By the time all of their family had gathered, the musicians were beginning to play in preparation for the first set. Mr. Collins led Elizabeth to the line of dancers, smiling in his obsequious way. When the music started, any hopes she had harbored for an enjoyable set were destroyed. Mr. Collins, tall and heavy as he was, could not dance. It was not that he made a few missteps. It was that he did not appear to know his right from his left, turned the wrong way every single time, and stomped his heavy foot on hers whenever he got close enough. She was humiliated. Making it worse were his hints that he intended to stay close to her all night.

At the end of the set, he put clarity to his words by doing just that, sitting down next to her at the side of the room until he was suddenly recalled to his duty to his other cousins and asked Mary for the next set. Such was Elizabeth's embarrassment at his antics that she was relieved when Mr. Darcy came to claim his set, as she knew at least that her toes would not suffer for his efforts.

Elizabeth had not expected much from Mr. Darcy beyond expert dancing. She knew him to be taciturn, and so was prepared for no more than a stilted, brief conversation. She was surprised, therefore, when the gentleman engaged her in a stimulating conversation about the war with France, which he knew she followed from her time at Netherfield, succeeded by a discussion about the poems of William Cowper.

Near the end of the second dance of the set, Elizabeth ventured to comment, "I am surprised, Mr. Darcy, that you should take so much trouble to converse with me. I am aware of your general dislike of the company you are surrounded by, and I certainly know you do not find me worth your time and effort I must wonder to what end you exert yourself this night."

Having just been given the perfect opening, Darcy did not waste the opportunity, "I do indeed have a motive. I would like to request a word with you, if you please." He searched the room as the music ended. Spotting two empty chairs in a far corner of the room, he said, "There, in the back of the room, is a place we can sit and talk. We will be within sight of everyone in the room yet have a small degree of privacy." So saying, he did not give her the chance to decline, but took gentle hold of her elbow and steered her in the direction he wished her to go. Elizabeth was astonished at his audacity in directing her but was too well-bred to make a scene. She tried

74

to unobtrusively remove her arm from his grasp but was unsuccessful. All she could do was follow along.

Arriving at the chairs he had selected, he assisted her to sit and then placed himself in the adjacent chair, turning it a bit so that he faced her when seated. He was silent for a few minutes, staring at his hands clasped in front of him and gathering his thoughts. Elizabeth was just about to say something to him and take her leave when he began.

"You may have noticed, Miss Elizabeth, that I have paid you a great deal of attention over the course of our acquaintance." At her nod, he continued, "What has drawn you to my attention is your honesty. You are never less than polite with anyone; indeed, your manners are perfection itself. Yet, there is a difference in the way you treat your favorites from those who are not. I am aware, of course, that I am not counted among those favored few."

Decisions and Consequences

He had looked back down at his hands while he was speaking, but now looked up to see her looking at him warily. "You see, I am looking for a wife, I have a list of qualities I am looking, and you meet all of them. I believe we are a good match and can have a good marriage. I will be faithful to you, and expect you to be faithful to me, of course. What I am asking, Miss Elizabeth, is if you will marry me."

By the end of his speech, Elizabeth was in shock. She had never expected such a thing from this man. Indeed, she had not looked for a proposal from anyone, for she had not met a man she could both admire and respect as of yet. Still, she recognized the honor of it all. She resolved in her heart to let him down as gently as possible.

"I thank you, sir, for the honor of your proposal. I am afraid, however, that I must decline it."

Darcy had been prepared for this eventuality, knowing the lady as he did. "Have you already promised yourself to your cousin Collins, then?" He needed to be sure of this before he proceeded, not that it would stop him from marrying her. He had happened to overhear the man boasting to her sister of his engagement to Elizabeth during their dance. He had a half-formed plan in mind, in case she had already accepted him.

At first, Elizabeth laughed at the notion that she would agree to marry her toad of a cousin, but as she thought about it more, she began to get angry. "No indeed! Mr. Collins has not asked me to marry him! Where did you get such a notion?" Elizabeth was angrier now that anyone would think she would marry Collins than uncomfortable with the proposal of marriage from a man she did not like.

Decisions and Consequences

"I overheard him speaking of it to your sister as they danced near us just now."

"Well, I never...I can assure you, Mr. Darcy, that I am not engaged to my cousin, nor do I ever intend to be. I wish to marry a man I can esteem and who I respect. Not a haughty man from the North and not an obsequious toad from Kent!" She made to rise and march away, but Darcy reached out a hand to stay her.

"Surely you can see the advantages of a match with me, Miss Elizabeth. I do respect you. Your mind is one of the finest I have come across and I have greatly enjoyed our debates and discussions. One does not need to like a person to respect them, would you not agree?"

Grudgingly, she responded, "I suppose you are right, in a way. One must give respect to certain persons regardless of our feelings about them. Governesses, for example."

"Yes, a very good example. So while we do not think very highly of each other at the moment, would you not agree that perhaps we may come to like each other at some point?"

"And should that never happen? What then, Mr. Darcy? What if one of us should meet someone we love? Are we to be doomed to merely like for the rest of our lives and do without the stronger emotion? No, the risk is too great. Again I thank you, but I must decline." Standing, she hurriedly curtseyed and strode away.

Darcy was not injured by her repeated dismissal of his hand. He was certain enough of his information that he knew he would win.

~~~***~~~

The next morning, to Elizabeth's dismay, Mr. Collins asked for a private audience with her that her mother insisted she grant. As she listened to his ridiculous words, she reflected that only she would ever receive two proposals in less than twelve hours. She certainly hoped there was another one in her future, or she would surely end an old maid. Her attention was forced back to her cousin when he began making assumptions in regards to her acceptance.

"As you know, Miss Elizabeth, I came to Longbourn to heal the breach between my family and yours, and to make amends to you and your sisters." He paused as if waiting for her to thank him for his beneficence, but when no words were forthcoming, for she had vowed to say nothing until he was done, he continued. "Almost from the first day I entered the house, I singled you out as the companion of my future life. Lady Catherine is certain to approve of your economy and good manners, and your liveliness and wit will surely be tempered by the awe her station will inspire in you. As to the matter of fortune, I

80

assure you the matter will never be mentioned again once we are wed. Let me tell you now of the violence of my affection and," he reached for her hand, but when she snatched it away, he stopped with a look of surprise and withdrew his, "ask you to be my wife."

"I thank you for the honor of your proposal, Cousin, but I must decline. I do not believe we suit. You could not make me happy and I am certain I could never make you so."

To her dismay, this rejection did not seem to penetrate his brain, and he prattled on another few minutes, reiterating the quality and prestige of his situation as a clergyman with a valuable living and his status as heir to her father's estate. Finally realizing that he was trying to convince her with his continued rattling on, she forcefully stated, "My answer is 'no,' Mr. Collins. I will not be swayed by your admirable situation or your condescending patroness. No, I will not marry you!" She then turned and exited the house as quickly as she could.

Unbeknownst to her, while she was conducting her private audience with Mr. Collins, her father was doing likewise with Mr. Darcy. Darcy had arrived while the majority of the family was still breaking their fast. Mr. Bennet, who had been walking across the entrance hall to his bookroom when the visitor arrived, took him immediately in and offered him refreshments. While waiting for tea to arrive, the two had exchanged pleasantries. Mr. Bennet could not for the life of him think what might entice a gentleman like Darcy to Longbourn. He was grateful his wife did not know the man was in the house, and he had instructed Mrs. Hill to keep it from her mistress.

Once their beverage had arrived and been served and they were left alone, Darcy got immediately to the point of the visit.

"I would like your permission to marry your daughter, Elizabeth."

Bennet choked on his mouthful of tea, causing a coughing spell of a few minutes' duration.

"Lizzy? You want to marry Lizzy? The one who was not handsome enough to tempt you?"

Darcy blushed a bit at that one. "At the risk of sounding crass, sir, she is definitely handsome enough to tempt me. The night I met Miss Elizabeth I was in a foul mood and wanted nothing more than for Bingley to leave me be. I am sorry she overheard me, but rest assured, she made sure I was aware of her thoughts on the matter."

Bennet chuckled. He could well imagine what she said. "And yet you still want her. Why? What has she, the daughter of a country squire and low-level gentry, have to entice you to offer for her? And, why are you asking me? Should you not be asking her?" He was starting to enjoy this conversation a great deal.

"I have asked her, and she turned me down. However, I want her. I admire her honesty, among other things. I have been searching for a wife for a long time and have made a list of attributes to look for. Your daughter has every item on the list.

"She is accomplished; I have heard her performance on the pianoforte and find it charming, she embroiders, she knows her languages, and her manners are impeccable. Most important of all, she is honest in her dealings. She maintains her countenance even when dealing with those she does not care for, whose company she would rather avoid. I have witnessed her tenderness with those she does love—you and your eldest daughter, for example. I believe she would make a perfect mistress for my estate. I am well able to care for her and will grant her a large settlement. I will take her with me when I travel; she can see the world, should she so choose. Of course, I also require an heir, so there will be times she will need to remain at Pemberley or in my townhouse in London. However, her sphere will be greatly expanded, and I will have a wife I can trust. In my eyes, it is a good solution for both of us."

"I am impressed, sir, that you noticed so much about my daughter. Yes, she would enjoy travel and expanding her knowledge of the world. She is the one of my offspring who has craved learning the most. It would be advantageous to her. However, she turned you down and I will not force her. It must be her choice. I do not wish to condemn her to a life where she is not equal to her partner."

"You do not wish your daughter to have all the advantages possible?"

Decisions and Consequences

"Oh, I do, but I also wish for her to be equal in marriage. I want her to have a partner she can respect and who respects her in turn."

"I do respect her, and I will. She has much to offer, and will be a credit to me, as she is to you. Surely you can see that I am the best choice for her? She will likely never meet another of my consequence who will offer for her." Mr. Darcy continued arguing his case for the next quarter hour. Finally, feeling like he was making no headway at all, he gave in and pulled out his trump card.

"I was just as certain you would deny me as I was that Miss Elizabeth would reject my suit. With that in mind, I had my solicitor do some research into you, your family, and your estate."

Mr. Bennet sat up in alarm at this. He was angered at the man's presumption, and dreaded his findings, knowing they could change his life as he knew it.

"It would seem, Mr. Bennet, that Longbourn is entailed upon your cousin, Mr. Collins." When Bennet nodded, Darcy continued. The look in the older man's eyes was enough to tell him that his strategy was going to work. "Mr. Collins is the rector of Hunsford Parish, correct?" At Mr. Bennet's nod, he forged ahead, "His patroness is my aunt, Lady Catherine de Bourgh."

"Yes, we have certainly heard much about her."

The corner of Darcy's mouth turned up in a small smile. "I am sure you have. I have heard your cousin's effusions about her myself, at the ball last night." He paused for a moment, then continued, "My solicitor is certain that Mr. Collins is unaware of a particular codicil in your father's will. His father must also have been uninformed or he would have told his son." He pulled a folded packet of papers out of his inside coat pocket, opened them up,

Decisions and Consequences

and began reading the contents aloud. When he was finished, he added, "It would seem, Mr. Bennet, that you have defied your father's wishes by marrying the current Mrs Bennet. Should Mr. Collins discover this information, he could force you and your family to remove yourselves from Longbourn and take it over. I am prepared to hold this information, keeping it to myself, so that you may continue on here as you have been."

Mr. Bennet was by now in a highly agitated state. Anger at this man's presumption warred with fear of the consequences, should that information reach Collins' ears. "Lizzy could marry Collins, or any of my girls could, and the point would be moot, sir."

"You would not force Miss Elizabeth to accept me; why should you force her to accept him? You have seen with your own eyes his obsequiousness and stupidity.

88

Would you not rather have your favorite daughter, and I have been assured she is your favorite, married to a man who would respect her and inspire that feeling in turn than to one who does not respect her at all?" He paused again, watching the man on the other side of the desk as he weighed his options. He was about to speak again when Mrs. Bennet suddenly burst into the room.

Chapter 4

"Mr. Bennet! You must come immediately!" She did not appear to notice the gentleman in the room with her husband.

"I have not the pleasure of understanding you. Of what are you speaking?" Mr. Bennet, while annoyed at her invasion of his private domain, was glad for the distraction. He did not like his dirty laundry aired, not even in private.

"You must come make Lizzy marry Mr. Collins! He has proposed and she says she will not have him. If you do not hurry, he will change his mind and not have her, then who will maintain her when you are gone? I will not have the funds; that is certain!"

"Lizzy has turned down a proposal from my cousin?" Mr. Bennet's

91

mind began to turn, seeing a possible way out of his dilemma. "Well, my dear, all hope is not lost. Send her in." As his wife scurried out the door to collect Elizabeth, Mr. Bennet looked to Darcy. "It seems my second daughter has turned down two proposals in as many days. Well Mr. Darcy, you may be in luck. I shall leave it to Lizzy to decide who she will marry. I will insist she choose one of you. What say you?"

Darcy replied, "I am confident enough in my words last night, sir. I am certain she will choose properly."

Bennet snorted. "Choose you, you mean."

Just then, the door opened to Mrs. Bennet and Elizabeth, followed closely by Mr. Collins, who was still endeavoring to change his cousin's mind. The men inside the room stood, and Elizabeth's eyes widened as she took in the visitor. Mrs. Bennet, too, finally noticed him.

"Mrs. Bennet, please make Mr. Darcy comfortable in the drawing room. Mr. Collins, you may follow them out. I care not where you go, just go for now. I wish to speak to my daughter alone."

Once everyone was gone and the door closed, he turned to his favorite child. How he hated the position he was now in! To force her to choose between two men she disliked, to tie herself to one of them for the rest of her life, was not something he ever imagined he might have to do. He sat beside her on the settee and took her hand gently in his.

"My child, your mother informs me that you have turned down a proposal this morning from Mr. Collins. Is this so?"

"Yes, sir."

"And Mr. Darcy, as you saw, was here this morning to inform me that he has also proposed, and you turned him down, as well. Is he correct?"

Decisions and Consequences

"Yes, sir, but—"

"Shh, wait before you speak, my child. Lizzy, an unhappy alternative is before you. Your mother insists you marry Mr. Collins, and Mr. Darcy has uncovered information that may cause us to be thrown out of Longbourn, should you choose against him. If you marry my cousin, you and he will certainly stay here and there is hope that he will allow us all to remain once Mr. Darcy reveals all to him. If you marry Darcy, the information he has discovered will remain hidden and your family will remain as it always has, here at Longbourn. He promises a generous settlement for you, and I will make sure a clause is added guaranteeing the information he holds is hidden away or destroyed. I will not force you to marry one over the other, but you do have to choose one. There is no other option."

Elizabeth was flabbergasted. "What possible information could he have that would result in such a thing?" she demanded. Her father would not tell her. No matter how she begged, pleaded, or cajoled, he could not be budged from his silence. After a full half an hour, she gave up.

"So I must choose one?" At her father's nod, she gave serious consideration to her options, all the while knowing there really was no choice. She could not bear the thought of being tied to Mr. Collins for all eternity. She may not like Mr. Darcy very much, but he was intelligent and had offered her respect. He had so much more to give her in the way of knowledge and a happy life. She would be able to travel, as she had always wished to, and would have access to more books and even masters to teach her things. She would also be exposed to a more educated society, where

Decisions and Consequences

she could put her knowledge and language skills to the test, attending salons and debates and displays. If she chose Collins, there would be none of that. It would be stifling.

"Very well. I choose Mr. Darcy. I would rather know I will be given greater opportunities to learn than be limited in my activities, as I know Mr. Collins would do. But I am not happy. I would have you know that."

Mr. Bennet nodded. He was relieved to have gotten out of the interview without giving his secret away. "I am sorry, Lizzy. This is not how I ever imagined one of my daughters leaving me. But it has happened and nothing can be done. I believe you have made the better choice. I believe he likes you more than any of us realized, and I have hope that you will be happy in the end. Certainly, you will be happier with him than with my heir."

Elizabeth nodded. There was nothing she could say, so she did not try.

"Go, my child, your betrothed awaits you in the drawing room. Send your mother in that I may tell her the news myself. I will endeavor to keep her effusions contained to this room for as long as I can."

"Thank you, Papa." She hesitated a moment, before leaning over to kiss him on the head and walk out of the room.

Upon entering the drawing room, she saw Mr. Collins, who had by now realized that this Mr. Darcy was the very one who was nephew to his patroness, alternately bowing and speaking urgently to him. She caught Mr. Darcy's eye, and that was enough for him to take action.

"Mr. Collins," Darcy began, "I thank you for your information about my aunt and cousin." Finishing his sentence, he rose and bowed to Elizabeth.

Decisions and Consequences

"Mama," Elizabeth began speaking as soon as she completed her curtseys to the gentlemen. "Papa requires your presence in the bookroom."

Mrs. Bennet was not accustomed to being asked to join him in that manner, and her curiosity was great. She hoped it meant that Lizzy was being forced to make the correct decision. She immediately rushed out of the drawing room to make her way to her husband.

The two gentlemen were left standing, looking after her. Elizabeth was amused for a moment at the thought that both of these men had asked for her hand. She was at peace with her decision, which made the words she was about to speak easier to say.

"Mr. Darcy, Mr. Collins, you both have asked for my hand in the last day."

At this, Collins looked in shock and surprise at Mr. Darcy, wondering when the gentleman had found opportunity to speak to the lady.

Elizabeth continued, hoping her cousin was paying attention. "I have been informed by my father that I must choose one of you. After careful consideration, I have chosen Mr. Darcy. I am sorry, Mr. Collins, for your disappointment and that of your patroness. You both would have been an excellent choice, but Mr. Darcy has more to offer."

Mr. Collins was in shock. She rejected him again! "But—," he spluttered.

"Mr. Collins," began Darcy in a stern voice, "the lady has made her decision and it was not in your favor. The proper course for you is to graciously thank her for her con-sideration and leave. She and I have much to discuss."

At the words of the rival he did not even know he had, who was possessed of so much more conse-quence than he could ever aspire to,

Decisions and Consequences

Mr. Collins' mouth snapped shut. He would have liked to argue further, for he was still left without a wife-to-be, but obedience to his betters was ingrained in him, so he immediately bowed and turned, leaving the room with haste. He would need to think about whom else to ask, for he dared not displease his patroness by arriving at Hunsford unengaged.

In the drawing room, Darcy had taken Elizabeth's hand in his own, bestowing a kiss on the back. As fast as his heart raced at her touch, hers did the same, causing a light blush to overtake her features. Darcy was heartened by this, as it indicated that felicity in the physical part of their marriage was likely.

He pulled her toward him, settling her on the couch where he had been sitting and himself beside her. "We must begin making plans, my dear," he began.

"Before we do, I would like to know what it is you are holding over my father's head to alarm him so. He would not tell me."

"If he will not, then I will not. It is not my tale to tell, and I have sworn myself to secrecy. No one will ever hear his story from my lips."

Elizabeth narrowed her eyes at him. She was unhappy with the entire situation, but she did not yet know how Darcy could be worked upon and, therefore, had to be content with what little knowledge she had. *Which really is none,* she thought.

To him, she said, "Very well. What do you wish to discuss, Mr. Darcy?"

"To start with, when we are alone, I should like you to call me by my first name, which is Fitzwilliam. I do not wish us to always be so formal with each other. I believe we are going to be able to reach a high level of intimacy, and I wish to begin fostering it now."

"As you wish. You may call me Elizabeth, or Lizzy if you prefer."

"Do many call you by your full name?"

"No, not amongst my family and very close friends."

"Then I shall call you Elizabeth."

She nodded in response to his statement and waited for him to continue.

"I know that you are displeased with me, and possibly your father, right now, and you might wish for a long engagement. However, I would prefer to wait just a short time. My preference would be a fortnight, but it occurs to me that your mother would have very little time to prepare and that might cause undue stress on your father's household. Therefore, I suggest we marry just after the new year, but before Twelfth Night."

Elizabeth nodded, relieved that she had a few weeks to accustom herself to the changes. It did not hurt that her Aunt and Uncle Gardiner were due to arrive in a few more days, to spend the holidays with them. She would be able to consult her dearest relation, a thought that gave her great comfort.

"That sounds like an excellent plan."

"Very good. I will need to speak to your father once more before I leave today, to get details to include in your settlement. I will send an express to town to my solicitor, but will not need to go myself. When the papers are complete, he will bring them here."

Elizabeth nodded again. *He seems to be taking charge of a great many things,* was her first resentful thought. But then she realized that he wanted to give her mother time to plan, so clearly he did not intend to take charge of the whole event. She forced her ire down. There was no need for it yet.

"What are your plans, then, Mr...Fitzwilliam?" she asked.

He took hold of her hand once more, raising it again to his mouth. "I intend to use that time to get to know you better, and to discuss the myriad of details of our married life that need to be worked out ahead of time."

Her mouth dry, Elizabeth swallowed and croaked, "Details?"

Darcy leaned over closer to her, "Details, yes, such as the decoration of your chambers in our homes." Her scent was enticing, prompting him to lean closer and place his free hand at the back of her head, then close that small gap between his lips and hers.

As he kissed her ever so gently, Elizabeth was stirred to the center of her being. She felt electrified, like every nerve was standing on end. Before she knew what she was about, she was kissing him back, and when his tongue probed the area where her lips were joined, she opened to him, engaging him in a duel of sorts inside her mouth. Finally, as he slowed the kiss and she began to come back to her senses, she was left in wonder at such feelings, and for a man she was not fond of. She resolved to ask her aunt about them as soon as possible.

For Darcy, the kiss was equally moving. His greatest desire at that moment was to pull her into his arms and make love to her right there. He could not, of course, and so he began to draw away from her. He was heartened to know that she was so responsive, though, and was pleased that this aspect of their married life would be a happy one. Finally removing his lips from hers, he pressed his cheek against her head until his breathing was once again under control.

"I am pleased, Elizabeth, at your response to my kiss. I would wish you to always be so enthusiastic."

Elizabeth blushed. "It is not like me to be so wanton. Please forgive me."

"What happens between a husband and a wife is not wrong, so there is nothing to forgive. It is a relief to know that a passionate woman lies beneath your proper exterior. What happens between us when we are in private, whether in our chambers or locked in another room of the house, is our business. Nothing is sinful; you are not wanton to enjoy our intimacy and to instigate our play, and I am not a rake for asking things of you that will bring us pleasure. Do you agree?"

Taking a deep breath, Elizabeth solemnly responded, "I know nothing of what happens between a husband and a wife. I have faithfully followed the Church's teachings on what is proper and what is not.

However, I see the sense in your words. I will agree."

"Very good." He stood, holding his hand out to help Elizabeth rise. "I expect your mother to return in a few minutes. When she does, I will go and speak to your father about your settlement. I will write to my solicitor in town. He will bring the papers here himself, I am certain. I plan to ask him to retrieve the Darcy jewels and transport them to me, as well. I will choose a ring for you from the collection, but if you do not like it, you will be free to select another."

Elizabeth nodded. Still unsettled from her behavior and the feelings that had rushed through her during their kiss, she cared not about rings and settlements. Despite his words, Elizabeth had been taught for as long as she remembered that a proper lady did not behave in such a manner, much less enjoy those kinds of attentions from a man. *Another reason it is good*

107

Decisions and Consequences

Aunt Maddie and Uncle Edward are coming, she thought. *I can ask her for advice. I certainly will not be asking my mother about it!*

No further words were shared between the newly-betrothed couple, for at that moment, Mrs. Bennet burst through the door. "Oh, Lizzy, my darling child! How sly you are! I never for a moment thought you would attract such a man! Mr. Collins is nothing to Mr. Darcy!"

Elizabeth was deeply embarrassed at her mother's exclamations. She glanced at Darcy to see how he was taking it and was unsurprised to see a cold mask on his face. She wondered briefly if she would be required to give up her family after her marriage, but as her attention was needed to redirect her mother, she ignored him and spoke instead to Mrs. Bennet. "Thank you, Mama. I knew you would be pleased with my choice. If you are done speaking to Papa, perhaps Mr.

Darcy should go to him and begin negotiating my settlement?"

"Oh, indeed!" Mrs. Bennet's eyes widened as an eager smile spread across her face. "Mr. Darcy, sir, my husband is only reading, I am sure. You must go now before he gets too lost in the words and refuses to see you!"

"Thank you, Madam." Darcy bowed to his betrothed and her mother, then left the room. He was only too happy to escape Mrs. Bennet. The thought that he would be connected to such an uncouth woman made him shudder. He was happy for the distance between Longbourn and Pemberley and that the Bennets did not have much money for extravagances like frequent travel. He would not be required to be in her presence often.

Elizabeth spent the next hour patiently listening to her mother talk of wedding breakfasts and trousseaus and lace on gowns. She had no time to ponder the happenings of the morning. That would have to wait for night.

Eventually, her father and betrothed left the bookroom and came to the drawing room for tea. At that time, her mother pressed Darcy to stay for supper. While it was apparent that he did not relish the idea of spending that much time in the bosom of the Bennet family, he graciously accepted.

Later that night, as she prepared for bed, Jane knocked on her door. It was their habit to spend at least a few minutes together every night discussing the events of the day and their impressions of them.

"Lizzy," Jane began cautiously, "how is it that you are engaged to Mr. Darcy when it was Mr. Collins who proposed?"

Elizabeth sighed as she reclined on the bed next to her sister. "Mr. Darcy proposed at the ball last night and I turned him down. I had no idea he would come and ask Papa for my hand anyway." She paused, not able to look up as she debated how much to tell her kindhearted sister.

"Tell me," Jane encouraged when she realized Elizabeth's struggle.

Looking up from the bed and away from her sister, Elizabeth stared at the wall as she stated, "Mr. Darcy has something he is holding over Papa, some knowledge that, should it be made known, could result in us losing Longbourn. That is all either of them will tell me. I did everything I could to get it out of Papa, but he is not telling, and Mr. Darcy said that it was not his tale to tell and that if my father would not tell me, he would not either."

Jane was silent for a long moment as she tried to see something good in the situation. She was slightly alarmed by what she heard, for she could not imagine anything that could cause them to be re-

Decisions and Consequences

moved from their home. Finally, she asked what had sorted itself out as the most germane to the conversation so far, "You were forced, then, to agree to marry Mr. Darcy?"

"No, not forced. I could have chosen Mr. Collins and been practically assured that my family could stay. What I was given was not an ultimatum but a choice. I had received two offers of marriage and was told that I must choose one or the other. I was not to remain single. I must marry and it must be to one of them. So, I chose Mr. Darcy. He is, at least, intelligent and can offer me the advantage of increased learning. Mr. Collins would have made me lose my mind inside of a month, I am sure," she concluded with sarcasm.

"Dear Lizzy!" Jane held her sister's hand tightly. "Mr. Darcy must be a man of integrity if he refused to reveal the secret to you. I know you would not have chosen to marry him

112

in other circumstances, but surely this bodes well? You could not re-spect someone who was not honora-ble. You at least have the assurance that he is respectable."

"Yes," Elizabeth smiled weakly, "there is that."

Chapter 5

The day the Gardiners were scheduled to arrive, Elizabeth awoke eager to talk to her aunt. Impatiently she waited, refusing to even go walking, lest she miss the coming of her favorite and most reliable relative.

The last couple of weeks had been bizarre, in Elizabeth's opinion. Mr. Darcy had arrived each morning and stayed a large portion of the day. Each visit, he spent a few minutes with her father, generally a couple hours in the drawing room with her and her mother and sisters, and then took a long walk with her. Jane and Mr. Bingley chaperoned these daily excursions, using the opportunity to get to know each other better without Mrs. Bennet hovering over them.

Decisions and Consequences

The first few times, Mr. Darcy did most of the speaking, describing his estate at her request, and sharing details about his habits in town and at Pemberley, sometimes appealing to Bingley for confirmation or his opinion. She was relieved that, though he did attend a few society events, he was not one to get lost in the whirl of parties and balls for weeks on end.

Finally, after spending days describing her future lifestyle to her, Mr. Darcy began asking Elizabeth for her opinions and drawing her into deeper conversations. She was surprised to see that he attended to every word she spoke, and part of her wondered what he was about. Even more astonishing was that he recalled every preference she had indicated. She began to see that he truly did mean to respect her, at least for the time being. No one knew what the future held, of course, but it was a comfort to her that he made the effort now. As she considered the matter further, she began to feel that she should thank him for his attentiveness, in the hopes that by expressing her appreciation, she might encourage him to continue as he had begun.

"I must thank you, Mr. Darcy. Your willingness to hear my opinions and relieve my concerns gives me great hope for our marriage."

"You are welcome. I am glad I have been able to assure you on that point."

Elizabeth nodded her acknowledgment of his words, and they walked along silently for a while. She wanted him to know why she valued respect so much but was unsure if she should reveal the inner workings of her family to him. Finally deciding that he had witnessed several incidences that would confirm her words, and knowing that he was not an idiot and unable to understand what he had seen, she allowed the words to flow.

"It is just that I am a spectator every day to my parents' marriage, which is not built on mutual respect. It is one of the things I have feared most about our union. Though you assured me that would not be the case with us, it was not until very recently, when I realized that you pay attention to my opinions and concerns, that I came to understand that you mean to show me that which I crave so much."

"I am beginning as I intend to go on, Elizabeth. I expect you to respect me and be faithful to me; therefore, I must do the same to you."

Again Elizabeth nodded her assent and they continued on as they had before.

At some point during each walk, the couples became separated for a few minutes, and Mr. Darcy took advantage of that period of privacy to soundly kiss Elizabeth, who always responded. Even though their exchanges became rather passionate, Darcy always took care to stop before it was too late.

Elizabeth was embarrassed at her response to him in this area.

"I apologize, sir. I should not have behaved in such a wanton manner. I am ashamed. Please forgive me."

Mr. Darcy, who still held her tightly in his arms, chuckled a bit at her words. His body was raging with desire, and he was striving mightily to regain his composure.

"Do not fear, Elizabeth," he said as he lifted her chin so he could look her in the eye. "We are engaged to be married. It is perfectly normal and acceptable for a couple in our position to indulge in such actions. I have said before that it bodes well for us that you do respond so passionately to me. You are not wanton; I have said it before and I will say it again. Let me further assure you that we will not anticipate our vows, no matter how much one or both of us would like to. You have indicated that you appreciate being respected, and this is just another area where I am able to do so. Please do not trouble yourself further about it."

Despite his words to her, she was ashamed of her physical reaction to someone she did not like very much. She had always thought one must be madly in love with someone to desire them, and it confused her to have those feelings now.

And so here she was, in the window seat of Longbourn's drawing room, watching for her Aunt Maddie and Uncle Edward. Mr. Darcy had stayed at Netherfield today, not wanting to add to the uproar that was sure to develop upon their arrival. Elizabeth was glad for it. He disconcerted her more than she liked. She wanted to be able to relax into the presence of her most beloved family members and take advantage of the first moment she could get alone with her aunt.

That moment finally came shortly before dinner, when Mrs Gardiner, who had heard of Elizabeth's engagement with astonishment, asked her niece to assist her with something upstairs. Highly relieved to finally have the opportunity to be alone with her, Elizabeth eagerly agreed. Once in the privacy of her aunt's bedchamber, the two settled into the chairs in front of the fireplace.

"Now, Elizabeth," Mrs. Gardiner began, "tell me how this engagement came about. From your letters these last weeks, I had not imagined ever hearing such a thing between you and Mr. Darcy. Why, you could have knocked me over with a feather when your mother informed me!"

"Oh, Aunt, I never thought anything like this would happen, either! But the betrothal is not the thing that bothers me the most. There is more. First, though, let me tell you how I came to be engaged."

Elizabeth explained it all to her aunt, from Mr. Darcy's rejected proposal to Mr. Collins' and the entirety of her conversation with her father when he informed her that she must choose one.

"I think you were wise, my dear, to choose Mr. Darcy. Your opportunities with him will be far greater. I know of his family, and in my youth, I had the privilege of meeting his mother. His parents were both highly thought of in the town I lived, which is not far from Mr. Darcy's estate of Pemberley. I do not know what kind of a person he is, but I will write to my friends there and ask what they know of him. They do not travel in his circle, of course, but his reputation will be known." Mrs. Gardiner paused, looking carefully at her niece. "But I think perhaps there is something more on your mind than your betrothed's character?"

Elizabeth nodded. "Yes, Aunt Maddie, there is." She twisted her hands together as she stared at them in her lap. "I do not know how to even begin, so I will just say it." She paused, and seeing her aunt's nod, continued, "I have told you that I do not like Mr. Darcy, and that I chose him because I felt that I could live with him the rest of my life and not run mad. The lines were clear in my mind about him until...." She trailed off for a moment and looking back down, blurted out, "He kissed me. He kissed me and I liked it. I...I kissed him back. I was so wanton!" Her hands flew to her face as she turned red at the memory. "I never thought I could behave in such a manner! Oh, Aunt Maddie, what is wrong with me? I thought one had to be in

123

love to feel desire, but I do not love him, and still I find myself *wanting* to kiss him, and more!"

Madeline Gardiner felt a laugh rise within her but knew that Elizabeth would not appreciate levity at this moment. She truly was distressed by her feelings, and Mrs Gardiner knew the young lady would not get answers from her mother. "Oh, Lizzy," she began, "all is well! You are engaged to be married and are a young and healthy woman. There is nothing unnatural about wanting to be kissed by your betrothed. You are not wanton."

"But I do not love him!"

"Not now, but you may come to love him. There are many couples of all levels of society who do not marry for love. Frequently, more material concerns are the basis for marital unions. Security for the woman is one, as is the addition of dowries to the husband's business or estate coffers. I have heard of marriages among peers that were formed for political reasons, to ensure the backing of one family for another's work in Parliament, and even to form a solid alliance to get legislation passed. Amongst my own friends and acquaintances in trade, many young tradesmen marry the daughters of those in similar or complementing businesses with an eye to expanding. Many times, the young couple barely knows each other, yet the majority come to be fond of each other, if not outright in love."

"How, Aunt Maddie? How does this happen? How is it possible to give yourself intimately to someone you do not know?"

"Oh, anything is possible if one puts their mind to it. You have a better beginning than some of these women we speak of. You at least desire your betrothed. That will make the intimate part of your marriage much easier." She paused to gather Elizabeth's hand

Decisions and Consequences

in her own. "Lizzy, you are obviously aware of what the church teaches about marital relations, and you are a good girl. You would never disregard your upbringing, and so I believe that you are mature enough to hear what I am about to say. I would not tell the younger girls what I am about to share with you because their curiosity might get the best of them and lead them astray. When a woman shares her body with her husband, they are considered to be one flesh. Do you know why?"

"Because they have joined together to make a child?"

"Yes, they have joined together and a child could very well result from it. But the couple has not just joined together physically. There is a spiritual joining that occurs, as well. A tie is formed between them. I know that many people do not understand this. Many men, especially men of means, think nothing of visiting courtesans. Not that women do not have affairs. They do." She paused then to gather her thoughts. "It is just that I do not want you to continue to feel guilty, as I am sure you do, for desiring your husband-to-be while you do not think much of him. I am certain that once you get to know him better, your esteem for him will rise, and once the two of you have been intimate, there will be a tie between you that will make it even easier for you to fall in love. He is coming to dine, is he not?" At Elizabeth's nod, she added, "Then I will observe him. I promise that if I feel he is not a good match, I will speak to your uncle about it and see what can be done." She squeezed her niece's hand once more. "How does that sound?"

"Thank you, Aunt Maddie. That sounds wonderful. You have given me much to think about. Thank you for listening without judgment. I will do my best to accept that these feelings are natural."

"Excellent! Now, give me a hug before you go. I will be down as soon as I freshen up a bit."

That evening, Mrs. Gardiner was as good as her word, examining Mr. Darcy and his interactions with Elizabeth and the rest of the guests, and engaging him in conversation.

"I understand you are from Derbyshire, Mr. Darcy?"

"Yes, madam, I am. Are you familiar with the area?"

"Oh, yes! I spent part of my youth there, in Lambton."

Mr. Darcy nodded. "Lambton is quite close to my estate, Pemberley."

"Yes, I remember visiting once, at Christmas. What a beautiful place! I remember your mother greeting us in the ballroom after our tour. She was the most beautiful lady I had ever seen, and so gracious to us all. I was saddened to learn of her passing."

"Thank you. She was very beautiful, and lively when amongst family. My father said, though, that she was shy with strangers. He has passed now, as well."

"I had heard that. I am so sorry, sir."

"Thank you. I miss them both, but I still have my sister, and now I will have a beautiful wife of my own." He looked to Elizabeth with a smile.

"Indeed. My niece is very like your mother in that she has an inner beauty as well as an outer one." She smiled at Elizabeth, then turned back to Mr. Darcy. "Would you tell me of your sister? Does she take after your mother, or is she more like your father? She is younger than you are, is she not?"

Mr. Darcy was always eager to praise his sister, and so they passed the next while discussing Miss Darcy and her accomplishments. Mr. Darcy was pleased to find both Mr. and Mrs. Gardiner were well-bred people with pleasing manners. *It would not be a punishment to spend time with them,* he thought to himself.

For her part, Mrs. Gardiner was pleasantly surprised to find Mr. Darcy an agreeable, if somewhat proud, gentleman. While he expressed no fond feelings for her second niece, his eyes followed Elizabeth everywhere she went. Mrs. Gardiner was certain he was perfect for her. If she was not mistaken, Mr. Darcy was well on his way to being in love with Elizabeth already. She was looking forward to the morrow, when she would report her findings to her niece.

Elizabeth left her aunt's room after their conference feeling much better about her engagement in general and her feelings of desire for her betrothed in specific. It was a relief to know that her feelings were normal. She realized now that she would have to change her thinking from that of a maiden to that of a married woman, as the expectations for each were different. She had been ambivalent about having rela tions with Mr. Darcy, given her lack of affection for him However, she was now determined to allow him his due in the privacy of their chambers. She recalled his words about the topic the first time he kissed her. He had been pleased that she was responsive to him. She hoped their marriage would be the better for it.

Elizabeth hoped, too, that Aunt Maddie was correct about a tie existing between a married couple. She did not want to spend the rest of her life disliking her husband. She must find something to like about him, beyond his intelligence and his circumstances which would broaden her horizons and expand her knowledge. She hoped she could grow to love him. She could

Decisions and Consequences

wait to hear what her aunt's friends
had to say about him, but she knew
she needed to know sooner than
that. For the entirety of the engagement, short though it was, she
had avoided questions that would
reveal his character. She determined that she would begin asking
them the next time they walked out.

Late that night, as she readied
herself for bed, Jane knocked on her
bedroom door. Hearing Elizabeth's
voice bid her to enter, she came in
and sat on her sister's bed, ready for
their nightly chat.

"Lizzy," she began, "Did you
speak to Aunt Maddie about your
concerns? Was she able to set your
mind at ease?"

"Yes, thankfully, she did. She
gave me much to think about.
While I did not wish to be in the position I currently find myself, I am
more at peace with it now."

"I noticed you and Mr. Darcy
were talking to each other today.

That is quite a change from the last weeks."

Elizabeth sighed, wondering if she would be able to verbalize to her sister what her aunt had told her. "I realized today that for us to have any semblance of a happy and fulfilling marriage, I must find something to like about him, beyond just the reasons I gave you for my choice. Aunt made me see that it is not the end of the world to marry someone for reasons other than love. I was given a choice between two men, and I feel I chose wisely. It is now up to me to see to my own happiness."

"This is true, my dear sister. What else did our aunt have to say? I know you have been concerned about doing your duty by him."

Blushing, Elizabeth nodded. "Yes, I have been. I believe I told you several days ago about the kisses Mr. Darcy has given me and how I have felt about them?"

Decisions and Consequences

Jane nodded, encouraging her closest sister to continue.

"Aunt has given me to understand that many women give themselves to gentlemen, be they husbands or lovers or...others....that they do not love. All I have to do is put my mind to it," Elizabeth continued wryly. "She also gave me hope, though, that the reaction my body has when Mr. Darcy kisses me will bring me great joy in the marriage bed. We did not get into details, so I am still unsure what exactly happens there, but I have faith now that I will enjoy it. Certainly, Mr. Darcy indicated himself that he enjoys what he calls my "passionate responses" and has said that he has high hopes that we will be happy together."

"I know you will, dearest sister. From what I have observed of him, I can say I believe he is a good man, and a good match for you. And if you enjoy his kisses, imagine what else you might enjoy with him."

134

"Oh, Jane," Elizabeth said with a laugh, "you never see ill in anybody. And never you mind about his kisses or anything else! They are not up for discussion!"

The pair laughed together for a few minutes. When they had caught their breath again, Elizabeth asked, with a sly look at her sister, "And what of Mr. Bingley?"

"He has not kissed me yet, but I would certainly not mind if he did!"

This set the pair to laughing again, but Elizabeth was not to be deterred.

"It is too bad he could not come to supper this evening. Chaperoning Mr. Darcy and me has given you many opportunities to speak to each other. How is your romance progressing?"

"Our romance," Jane scoffed. "I am not certain we have one. I believe he likes me, and I most certainly think very highly of him, but he seems slow to act. I wish I knew why."

Thoughtfully, Elizabeth asked, "Do you think his sisters might be the cause?"

"Truthfully, I do not know. I have tried as much as I am able to show him my feelings. I do not wish to be like Lydia and wear them on my sleeve. I am a lady and I wish to behave as one." She sighed. "I can only hope it is enough."

"Charlotte said to me once that a woman ought to show more than she feels to secure a man, and that she feared you needed to give Mr. Bingley more encouragement. I disagreed with her then, because you barely knew him at the time. Now, however, you have had more time together. Does he seem genuine? Is he someone you could love? Are you certain of his character?"

"Oh, yes, I am certain. I believe he and I would be well-matched. We are similar in temperament and outlook. We desire the same things in life, family, and a home. Neither of us wishes to be in discord with anyone else. I enjoy his liveliness and he has said he likes my serenity. I do not wish to speak it aloud prematurely, but he is most definitely someone I could love." She hesitated, then went on, "Do you think that perhaps he does not recognize my encouragement for what it is? Is it possible he does not understand the depth of my regard for him?" Jane looked anxiously at Elizabeth, eager to hear her opinion of the matter.

"It is possible, I fear. The very serenity he enjoys could be a stumbling block to his understanding of you. But I know you, Jane. You are the very model of propriety in public. Will you be capable of showing him how you feel?"

Chewing her lip, Jane responded thoughtfully, "I do not know. I am not certain I know how to do so. Do you think Aunt Maddie might have some advice?"

"She may very well do so. You should seek an audience with her tomorrow. After, of course, she shares her impressions of my betrothed with me." Elizabeth winked at her and laughed.

"Oh, certainly. My paltry needs are nothing to yours, my poor, neglected sister." Jane winked back and once again the pair were lost in gales of laughter.

~~~***~~~

For Darcy, the first two weeks of his engagement only solidified his confidence in his decision to make Miss Elizabeth the Mistress of Pemberley. He had observed her many times as she masterfully handled her mother's overexcitement about the upcoming wedding, which had been set for the third day in January.

Darcy also, in the course of his visits, observed his friend and his soon-to-be sister. At first, it did not seem that Jane received any more pleasure in Bingley's company than in that of any other person. However, the longer Darcy spent in the presence of his betrothed's family, the more he was able to recognize a subtle difference between Jane's behavior toward Bingley and that she displayed to her family and the many friends that came to visit, including Bingley's sisters and brother-in-law. He came to realize that it was likely the eldest Miss Bennet welcomed the attentions of his friend and he began to wonder at Bingley's reluctance to move ahead with a relationship with a lady he obviously admired. The day before the Gardiners were due to arrive at Longbourn, he finally asked.

"Bingley," he began, uncomfortable with the question but curious to hear the answer, "I hope you do not mind my asking, but I have noticed that you and Miss Bennet have gotten rather close these last couple of weeks, yet to my knowledge you have not asked her for a courtship. Why is that? It is not like you to lead a lady on, and I am concerned that the Bennets might feel perhaps you are."

"I do not mind at all, Darcy. In fact, I was searching for a way to ask your advice on the matter."

"Well, ask away then."

"Thank you. I shall. You see, I am uncertain of Miss Bennet's feelings for me. She is very beautiful, and incredibly serene, both of which attract me. I had thought she liked me as much as I like her. We have taken advantage of our chaperone duties and learned as much about each other as we could. Her smiles for me seemed to be more than those she bestows on others."

"Yet?" Darcy prompted when his friend fell silent.

"Yet, Caroline assures me that Miss Bennet's heart is untouched."

He shook his head, "I was so certain of her, and was ready to ask for her hand. Caroline's words broke my heart, and she is my sister. She would not lie to me, not about something this important to me."

"Bingley, I am afraid she would lie to you." He paused. "You are aware that I am known as a keen observer, are you not?" At his friend's nod, Darcy continued, "I have seen the difference you spoke of in Miss Bennet's smiles to you compared to others of her acquaintance. I am certain she holds you in high esteem and that if you asked for her hand, you would receive it."

"But Caroline felt that if Jane accepted me, it would be at the behest of her mother and not because of her feelings for me. Then, too, Caro pointed out that the Bennets are not very high in society and a union with Jane would lessen her chances of marrying well."

Decisions and Consequences

"More lies, my friend. Jane Bennet's connections are about to be raised very high. She already ranks, and I apologize for my bluntness, higher than your sister. Marriage to her would only raise your consequence. As my sister, that connection is even more valuable, to both you and Miss Bingley. Your sister, my friend, does not like Mrs. Bennet and the younger girls, nor does she like the fact that I overlooked her in my search for a wife."

Bingley nodded as his eyes were opened to his sister's perfidy and his hopes were raised. "You are right. I can see now that she was being self-serving. In the back of my mind, I had hoped that was the case, but I was not sure. Thank you, Darcy, for bringing this up." He smiled. "We may soon be brothers! I could not ask for a better one," he exclaimed as he clapped Darcy on the shoulder.

With a smile, Darcy replied, "Indeed! I could say the same. Come, Brother, let us go out for a ride before it gets dark." Bingley eagerly agreed and they set off for the stables.

Chapter 6

The morning after the Gardiners' arrival, Darcy and Bingley arrived at Longbourn in time to break their fast with the family. Bingley went immediately to Jane's side and took the place that had become his. Darcy paid his respects to Mr. and Mrs. Bennet and Mr. and Mrs. Gardiner before he took a seat next to Elizabeth. The youngest Bennet daughters and the Gardiner children were still above-stairs. Darcy enjoyed the quiet, knowing it would not last. After they had eaten, he asked Elizabeth to join him on a walk, knowing that Bingley wanted to get Jane alone so he could propose.

"Yes, Mr. Darcy, a walk would be lovely. I will be happy to join you, if Jane and Mr. Bingley could come along?"

Decisions and Consequences

Bingley jumped up, "I would be happy to walk with you." Turning to Jane, he asked, "Miss Bennet, would you like to join us, as well?"

Smiling, Jane agreed, taking the hand he offered and rising from the chair. The four of them went to the entrance hall to put on their hats and coats and walk out into the sunny but cold morning.

As usual, the couples became separated during their excursion, and as usual, Darcy took advantage to kiss his betrothed. He looked forward to these moments. The feeling of his blood stirring was an addictive one, and he now had a greater understanding of why his peers were so eager to engage in sexual activities before, and sometimes outside of, marriage. Darcy was glad he had waited, though he could not clearly define why. It was true that Miss Elizabeth improved upon further acquaintance, but he did not love her.

In truth, the more he considered the matter, the more uneasy he became about his enthusiasm. He shoved it to the back of his mind most times, but the fact was that he was not sure he should feel desire for a woman he did not like. For the moment, however, she was before him and so once again, his trepidation was shoved aside for more immediate pleasures.

After enjoying a few minutes of passionate kissing, the couple stepped back out on the path and resumed their walk.

"Tell me, Fitzwilliam, your impression of my aunt and uncle. I know you were reluctant to make their acquaintance. I could see by your expression that you were surprised at them."

"I was surprised, I admit. Knowing your uncle to be your mother's relation, I expected someone very...different."

Decisions and Consequences

"You expected him to be brash and uncouth."

"Well, yes, I did," Darcy reluctantly admitted. "Had I not known otherwise, I would have taken your aunt and uncle to be people of fashionable society. I never would have dreamt they were tradespeople."

Elizabeth's smile was smug. "Are they sufficiently educated and fine that I will not have to give them up when we marry?"

Her statement took him aback. Did she think she must give up her family upon their marriage? Did he want to maintain a connection to any of them? He recalled being grateful on more than one occasion for the distance between Pemberley and Longbourn, and he acknowledged to himself that Mrs. Bennet was offensive to his sensibilities. *She is offensive to me,* he thought, *but she is Elizabeth's mother. Would I want Georgiana to have to give up a connection to any of her family members upon marriage? No, indeed; I would be highly offended at the suggestion. So, why have I done the same?* Darcy blushed as he began to realize the arrogance of his previous thoughts.

Elizabeth had begun to grow nervous at her betrothed's continued silence. She watched his face begin to flush and wondered what he was thinking. Finally, she could bear it no longer. "Mr. Darcy?"

Her voice startled him out of his thoughts. He cleared his throat and licked his lips before responding. "Please, call me Fitzwilliam." He looked to see her nod, then continued, "Of course we shall maintain the connection. I am very sorry to have given the impression that I wished to sever any of your connections. It is neither my intention nor my desire to separate you completely from those you love."

With a sigh of relief, Elizabeth responded, "Thank you. I had feared the worst. I have witnessed your reaction to my mother and youngest sisters and was certain we would never see them again after the wedding."

"I will admit that the behavior of certain members of your family leaves much to be desired, and that I am grateful that our family homes are so far from each other. But I would be offended were someone to require that of a member of my own family." He paused to gather his thoughts and then began again. "My aunt, Lady Catherine, likes to....arrange things to suit herself. In truth, she is known for intruding into the affairs of others, particularly her inferiors, and insisting they live their lives as *she* sees fit. I can well imagine someone from outside the family becoming offended by it enough to demand their new spouse give up that connection. I should not want that to happen to me; I must not ask it of others." He was surprised and comforted when Elizabeth laid her hand on his arm.

"I must also apologize for the arrogance that led you to fear such a thing. My parents, my mother especially, would be ashamed of me." He looked down at his feet as he continued, "There is no excuse for my behavior. I cannot apologize for my feelings, but I should have hidden them so as not to give you unease. 'Twas not gentlemanly of me to display them."

"I accept your apology, Fitzwilliam. I am well aware that my mother and sisters often give offense. I have excused it away until now, for the most part, but I do see how someone unfamiliar with my family and our neighborhood would look upon it from a different perspective and wonder at our suitability." Elizabeth kept her gaze focused on her surroundings as she softly continued, "In truth, I would not have blamed you if you had made me give them up. I would have been hurt and angry, but I would have understood." She looked at him then with a small, almost teasing, smile. "I will admit now that I am also relieved at the distance between your estate and Longbourn. With so much peace available to me, I may not know what to do with myself!" When Darcy laughed at her statement, Elizabeth joined in, glad that was settled and that her favorite relatives would continue to be part of her life.

~~~***~~~

Mrs. Gardiner had no opportunity that day to share her impressions of Mr. Darcy with her niece until late in the evening, as the family members readied for bed. Elizabeth listened to her impressions carefully, nodding her understanding in places and asking clarifying questions in others.

"I was quite impressed with him," Aunt Maddie began. "So handsome and gentlemanly! He bore rather well with your mother, you know, and for someone of his standing that is saying something. He does not have to. He could have gone to town until the wedding so he would not be forced to deal with her."

Elizabeth nodded vigorously at that, murmuring her agreement.

"He is very proud of his family and estate, but then, he should be. When you see it, you will understand. There is something special about that place. It has been a very long time since I was there, but I remember as though it were yesterday. It was very elegant. Unless the décor has changed since then, I think you will like it very much.

"Of course, he earned my good opinion with his actions toward you. He was so solicitous of your welfare! Did you hear him defend you to your mother?"

Decisions and Consequences

Elizabeth blushed at the memory. "Yes, I did."

"And his eyes! They followed you everywhere you went. He was speaking to me but his eyes were on you. That man is falling in love with you; mark my words!"

Elizabeth appreciated her aunt's observations, though she did scoff at the idea that Mr. Darcy was falling in love with her. "I can assure you, he is not. He appreciates my honesty and manners, to be sure, but he does not love me and I doubt he ever will." At Mrs. Gardiner's look, which could be best described as skeptical, Elizabeth added, "I remember what you told me, and I am open to the possibility of felicity between us once we have become intimate, but I cannot see his suddenly falling madly in love with me before that."

Shaking her head, Mrs. Gardiner simply replied, "Very well, darling, but do take care. A gentleman's heart is a fragile thing. If he offers it, no matter how poorly he words it, do not hurt him with your sharp tongue; for once it is broken, it will not mend easily. Now, I will close our discussion with that and leave you to your dreams. Good night, Lizzy." She kissed her niece's cheek, accepting a hug and kiss in return, then retired to her own chambers, where Mr. Gardiner awaited her.

~~~***~~~

The following day, when Darcy and Bingley arrived at Longbourn, there was a stranger with them, a man who, along with Darcy, went immediately to Mr. Bennet in the bookroom. Bingley relieved the curiosity of the ladies when he entered the drawing room and informed them that the man was Darcy's solicitor from London. He had arrived at Netherfield just after dark the day before with Elizabeth's settlement.

Decisions and Consequences

Mrs. Bennet was all aflutter at the news, for it was one step closer to her second daughter's security, and as she usually did, expressed her curiosity and excitement loudly and inappropriately.

Elizabeth was not sure how she felt about it all. While, on one hand, she was eager to see and be reassured of her future security, the settlement represented one more nail in the coffin of her maidenhood. She was distracted enough that, for once, she did not hear her mother's exclamations.

After an hour of waiting, sometimes anxiously and other times with trepidation, Elizabeth was called to the bookroom. As she entered, she took in the four men standing there, her father behind his desk, her uncle beside it, and her betrothed and the stranger in front. All four bowed in greeting as she entered and curtseyed. Finally, her father spoke.

"Mr. Franklin, may I present to you my second daughter, Elizabeth. Elizabeth, this is Mr. Franklin. He is Mr. Darcy's solicitor."

"I am pleased to meet you, sir."

"Likewise, Miss Bennet."

"Come sit, Lizzy," her father requested. "We have matters to discuss."

Elizabeth crossed the room, sitting in the chair placed there for her use between her father and uncle. Once she was seated and the men followed suit, Mr. Bennet cleared his throat and began speaking.

"Lizzy, Mr. Franklin has brought your settlement to me today. Your uncle and I have reviewed it carefully, and can find no fault with it."

Elizabeth nodded her understanding.

"I have signed it, as has Mr. Darcy. Mr. Franklin and Uncle Edward have signed as witnesses. The agreement is now binding, and I would have you understand what it says. You are an intelligent young lady, the most clever of all my daughters. I do not fear you ever turning into a replica of your mother, but I am aware that her lack of understanding contributes to her silliness, and I would not have you feel that you had to enter a marriage without comprehending what has been done to secure your future. If you have any questions, stop me and ask."

"Thank you, Papa, I will" she replied. Elizabeth was relieved to hear that her father respected her so much as to ensure she felt secure. It was not every father who would, she knew. She glanced at Mr. Darcy and his solicitor, wondering what they thought of it, and from the smile he granted her, understood that her betrothed was happy to reassure her.

At the end of the explanation, and after asking many questions to clarify her understanding, Elizabeth sat back in her chair, thoughts running rampant in her mind. She had not expected such a large amount of pin money, and no amount of protest seemed to change Mr. Darcy's mind. He insisted that it was no more than what his sister received, and that he was not entirely sure it would be enough and would not need to be added to. Unused to such large sums being at her fingertips, she wondered what she could possibly spend it on. She was assured, however, that as the wife of a gentleman of the first circles, she would require many gowns and accessories and would likely go through at least that much every year.

Then there was the amount he settled on her, should he die, and the dowries set aside for any number of daughters. Her girls would not have to share in a paltry sum upon her death, as she and her sisters currently did! Nor would she have to fear being thrown in the hedgerows. Why, Mr. Darcy even had small estates set aside to give younger sons! It was staggering the amount of wealth represented in her settlement. She began to see him in a new light as the reality of his responsibilities sank in. She looked at him with wide eyes as he spoke, concern evident in his expression.

"Miss Elizabeth, will you walk in the garden with me a while?"

"Yes, I should like that very much."

They left the bookroom through the glass doors set in the outside wall of the chamber. Once outside, Darcy offered her his arm. Elizabeth took it and they began a slow stroll along the paths. Darcy shot an anxious glance at her now and again, until his concern finally overrode his desire to allow her time to think.

"Are you well?"

She sighed. "Yes. I am contemplating what I have learned about you today."

"What is your conclusion?"

"I am not sure I have drawn one as yet." She stopped in the path, forcing him to stop, as well. "Just how many properties do you own?"

Darcy blushed. "Well," he sheepishly began, "besides the townhouse in London and Pemberley, there are five: small ones in Scotland and Yorkshire, and three slightly larger ones in Ireland, Wales, and Essex."

Elizabeth's free hand came to her chest to press there, as though she could still her heart. "Oh, my! I had no idea."

"I have housekeepers to run each of the smaller five houses. They are very efficient; you need not lift a finger if you choose not to."

"That is good, though I believe I am up for the challenge. My mother has trained all of her daughters to run a household. Regardless of size, the essentials are still the same."

Decisions and Consequences

"I have found that to be true with each of the estates, as well. Once one understands the basic methods, size does not matter. I am pleased that you are not overwhelmed by it all." *Just one more item that supports my decision to offer for you,* he added silently.

The couple continued along the garden paths for a while, each lost in their own thoughts. Unknown to the other person, each considered what they knew of the other.

Elizabeth, her eyes opened to the vast responsibilities her betrothed carried, began to see that perhaps he had good reason to be severe at times. On the heels of that thought was another; that she had seen him at Netherfield with a smile on his face or a chuckle on his lips. Certainly, he did not smile often, and never did he laugh outright. Still, he was not always serious and stoic. She felt that she liked him a little better now that she understood him better.

Darcy, relieved that Elizabeth did not seem intimidated by the amount and sizes of his properties, added confidence to his mental list of the qualities she possessed that made her a good Mistress of his homes. Recalling his affront when she made a joke out of him at the Meryton Assembly, he began to see that it was that assurance that allowed her to turn injurious statements back on those who made them, thereby deflecting the hurt intended by them. When he looked at the whole picture of who his betrothed was, he came to see that he liked her a little better now that he understood her better.

They continued on, walking as a couple but deep in their individual thoughts, for a further half-hour before being called in to dine. They did not speak, but neither felt un-

Decisions and Consequences

comfortable with the silence between them.

~~~***~~~

The very next day, Elizabeth and her sisters walked into Meryton. Darcy and Bingley were out shooting with Mr. Bennet and Sir William, and the ladies all longed for an outing. They called in on their aunt, Mrs. Phillips.

To their surprise, their aunt was entertaining some of the officers, whom she had invited to take tea with her and her husband. Among the officers present was Mr. Wickham. Although Jane and Elizabeth had not seen him since their walk to Meryton after Jane's illness, the three younger girls, Mary, Kitty, and Lydia, had seen them on several occasions. Mary, not being given to flirtations, ignored the officers for the most part. Kitty and Lydia, however, were enamored of them and never failed to stop and speak

164

to them. It was through the prattle of the two youngest Bennet ladies that Mr. Wickham learned of the engagement of his childhood friend, Darcy, to Miss Elizabeth Bennet.

Lieutenant George Wickham was the son of Darcy's father's long-time steward, John Wickham. The two boys had been raised together and were close as brothers as young boys. Darcy's father was George's godfather, and the boy enjoyed great favor as a result. They had grown apart as they grew, largely due to George's growing jealousy of all that Darcy was heir to. Sent to school together, first Eton and later Cambridge, the disparities in their personalities became pronounced. Darcy was studious and serious, but Wickham preferred carousing to learning. Many were the times Darcy was called upon to clean up or pay for Wickham's messes, which he always did. Although he was the heir, he knew his father preferred

Wickham. However, he loved his father enough to try to prevent any hurt or embarrassment.

Just as Darcy's days at University were coming to a close, he was called home to Pemberley. His father had fallen ill, and he was needed to make some decisions regarding the running of the estate. George Darcy lingered for several months, slowly getting weaker and weaker until one night he passed in his sleep. His son, who had assisted him for years, became Master in name as well as deed. John Wickham, who had caught the same illness as George Darcy, passed within six months.

When George Wickham arrived back at Pemberley for his father's funeral, he made application to Darcy for his inheritance from Darcy's father. Upon being told his legacy, which he had hoped would be a large sum of cash, consisted of one thousand pounds and a living, were he to take orders, Wickham was incredulous. He refused the living, taking in exchange the sum of three thousand pounds. He left Pemberley at that time and was not heard of again for two years.

When the living that had been designed for him came open, Wickham, who had run through his four thousand pounds and was in dire need of an infusion of funds, applied by letter for the position, reminding Darcy of his late father's wishes. His anger when he was refused was fearsome to behold. He reviled Darcy to everyone who would listen, and many did. His charm he used to great advantage.

Eventually, the idea of revenge became a plan. This past summer, one of his paramours, Mrs. Letty Younge, was hired by Darcy as his sister's companion. Georgiana was fifteen but looked older. At his instigation, Mrs. Younge convinced Darcy to send his sister to Ramsgate for the summer. Once there, Wickham began to pay attention to the girl, eventually convincing her that he loved her and that she should elope with him. He did not love her. Wickham had not loved anyone but himself since his mother died when he was ten. What he wanted was Georgiana's dowry, which was a hefty thirty thousand pounds.

Unfortunately for Wickham, Mrs. Younge, and their plans, Darcy arrived unexpectedly two days before the scheduled elopement. Georgiana, who loved her brother above anyone and desired him to share her joy, told him all. Within the hour, Mrs. Younge found herself unemployed without reference and Wickham had received a note at his lodgings demanding he leave the town immediately. Fearful of his prospects being further ruined by the angry Darcy, he did just that, without even trying to see the young lady again. Now even angrier than he had been, Wickham vowed to find another opportunity to get his due from the man he would from that day forth consider his enemy.

And now here he was in Meryton with Darcy's future wife in the same room. Wickham had spent the last two weeks concocting his scheme of revenge. He had been thrilled to hear from Miss Lydia that her elder sister was engaged to the man, even though she did not like him. Wickham was sure that if she heard his story, he would be able to thoroughly turn her against him. He laughed at the thought of Darcy tied for the rest of his life to a lady who hated him.

Chapter 7

Wickham was not an evil man, plotting death and destruction. He was a man, a gentleman in his own estimation, who took advantage of opportunities presented to him, and this was an exquisitely ripe one. The moment he saw Miss Elizabeth alone, he hastened to her side, his tale of woe at the ready.

"Miss Elizabeth, what a pleasure to see you again." Wickham bowed a greeting as he spoke, eyes alert to her every expression.

"Likewise, Lieutenant," Elizabeth replied with a smile. "My sisters have told me much about you."

"All good, I hope?"

"Nothing alarming, I assure you," Elizabeth laughed, settling back down into her seat. "How do you find Meryton, sir?"

171

"I find I like it rather well." Wickham sat in a chair beside hers. "I have received a most friendly welcome from my fellow officers as well as the residents of the town. I was quite delighted with the array of social events I have been invited to. I do love being part of society."

Elizabeth smiled; he was a likable fellow, this Wickham. She was glad to have an interesting person to converse with this evening. Not that the people she had known all her life were uninteresting. It was rather that she enjoyed having someone new to observe. The pair exchanged a few moments of chat when Wickham began to make her uneasy.

"How long has Mr. Darcy been in the area?"

Surprised at his question, Elizabeth answered readily. "I believe it has been more than two months."

"Ah, I see. Did he make himself agreeable to the neighborhood, or was he his usual standoffish self?"

After a pause, in which she considered how best to answer, Elizabeth replied, "At first, he was...quiet. None of us were very sure how to take him. He speaks more readily now, however, and I believe he has made some friends amongst the gentlemen of the area."

"And you are engaged to him?" At her nod, Wickham continued, "Your sister seems to think you dislike him. I wonder at your accepting him in that case. Perhaps it is his standing in society that attracts you?"

Elizabeth's lips tightened. She was becoming angry at his assumptions. "My sister knows nothing of my reasons for agreeing to marry Mr. Darcy. They were, and shall remain, my own."

Decisions and Consequences

"I did not intend to offend you, Miss Elizabeth. Please accept my apology."

At the sincerity in his expression, she nodded, letting go of her anger a bit, but determining to speak to her youngest sisters before much longer about what constituted proper discourse to a stranger.

Seeing her tension ease, Wickham began to speak again. "I feel it is my duty, Miss Elizabeth, to inform you of what your betrothed is like before it is too late." Her eyebrow rose, but she said nothing. He took this as permission to continue and launched into his story. He made sure to leave out anything that might put himself in a bad light and to embellish everything involving Darcy so that he appeared the villain. When he was finished, he looked expectantly at his companion.

For Elizabeth's part, the longer he spoke, the more astonished she became. The man Wickham spoke of in no way resembled the one she was getting set to marry. She considered herself an excellent judge of character, and while she was beginning to see that her initial evaluation of Darcy's nature had been in error, she was certain at this point, not far into her acquaintance with the lieutenant, that his initial congeniality was a cover for a devious mind. This alarmed her slightly, as she did not know him well enough to know what he might be capable of. She determined to get herself out of the situation as soon as possible and thought she should perhaps warn Darcy at the least. He should be made aware of what this man was saying about him.

As Wickham finished speaking, he could see that his companion had sunk into contemplation. He paused for a moment to determine his next course of action.

"I apologize, Miss Elizabeth. These are topics that tend to distress ladies. I should not have mentioned them."

Not wanting to give him an inkling of her true thoughts, Elizabeth smiled and assured him of her well-being. "Thank you for sharing this with me, sir. I promise you I shall give it a great deal of thought."

Just then, Lydia appeared at her side, fairly bouncing with excitement, for she had convinced Mary to play a jig. "Lizzy, you must give up Mr. Wickham to me. You have a gentleman of your own, and must not keep this one to yourself." Turning to Wickham, she grabbed his hand and pulled, "Come, Wickham, and dance with me."

With a sheepish grin at Elizabeth, he arose and followed her sister. Elizabeth remained, considering his tale and contemplating the reasons he might have for telling it to her. Suddenly aware that she was alone again and not wanting there to be another opportunity for him to get her by herself, she rose from her seat and removed to the other side of the room, where she planted herself beside her mother for the remainder of the afternoon.

That evening, Darcy and Bingley arrived to dine with the Bennets as they did every evening. They were early, as was usual. To Darcy's surprise, Elizabeth asked him to escort her through the gardens. This was the first time she had made any request of him for the entire length of their betrothal, to date. While he hoped it meant she enjoyed his kisses and wanted more, the look in her eyes indicated there were other things on her mind. Soon, they were outside, accompanied by Bingley and Jane, who dutifully fell behind so they could talk privately.

Elizabeth strode with purpose, and for once, Darcy was in danger of falling back. He repeatedly glanced at her. When they reached the bower he had utilized before for privacy

Decisions and Consequences

when he kissed her, she stopped. He stepped in front of her, pulling her into his arms; but instead of caressing her lips with his, he inquired after her.

"Is there something on your mind, Elizabeth?"

With a sigh, she admitted there was. Looking past his shoulder, then at the buttons on his waistcoat, she began speaking. "I met a man, a lieutenant in the militia, who claims an acquaintance with you. He told me a story about you, one I did not and do not believe, that does not match your character as I have come to know it. Why he would say such things, I do not know, but I do wonder at what else he might be capable of. I have eagerly awaited your arrival so I could tell you of him." She paused to gather her thoughts. "I do not know him well enough. For all I know, one or all of us might be in danger from him."

178

Darcy had gone from concerned but relaxed at her first words, to stiff and perturbed. "What was his name? What story did he tell?"

"His name was Wickham and he-"

"Wickham!" Darcy spat the name, his hold on his betrothed tightening. He looked down at her. "So that bounder has joined the militia? I wonder how he acquired the funds. Let me guess what he told you. He said I denied him a living?"

"Yes, he did, but I did not believe it. You could not disregard your father's wishes any more than you could cut off your right arm."

"Thank you for your faith in me. Let me tell you what really happened." Darcy spent the next few minutes telling the true tale of Wickham and his interactions with the Darcy family. Elizabeth was aghast that someone who called himself a gentleman would attempt to elope with the sister of a man to whom he was close as a brother. Surely he had known Georgiana Darcy as a young girl, had been close to her as a sister. The thought that he would attempt to elope with her made Elizabeth shiver in disgust.

"Oh, Fitzwilliam, I am so sorry! How is your sister now?"

"She is better, but her trust in her own judgment has been shaken. She will do well to have you for a sister. You did not fall all over me because of my wealth and status. You saw my rudeness for what it was and judged me, making certain I understood your opinion. Georgiana needs to be more like you. She needs to be less trusting, to learn to see the truth behind the facades that people wear, and not give her heart away so easily."

"You did not appreciate my judgment and I daresay you still dislike my method of expressing it."

"I did not, but upon reflection, I can understand why you made it. My mother would have been appalled at my refusal to dance when there were ladies sitting out. In that, you were correct. And, I do not wish Georgiana to be rude and ill-mannered, but neither do I want her to be overly complaisant."

"You cannot have it both ways, Fitzwilliam. She must be honest or complaisant."

Darcy rolled his eyes. "If you insist, Elizabeth. Let me attempt to clarify my position." He pondered a moment, deciding which words would be most effective in conveying his opinion. Coming to a decision, he stated, "I wish Georgiana to be perceptive enough to recognize the true measure of those she meets, wise enough to stay away from those who would use her, and mannerly enough to do it without causing offense to anyone."

Decisions and Consequences

It was Elizabeth's turn to roll her eyes. "Very well. She shall be a paragon, but perhaps you should think about replacing me in her life if that is what you wish, for a model of perfection I am not."

The couple had stood in an embrace while talking and now Darcy squeezed her tight. "Indeed not. I find the pleasure of your lips recompense enough for your impertinence." He leaned down to kiss her.

"Darcy! Where have you got to?"

"Blast!" Darcy muttered under his breath. "It seems I am to do without that pleasure today."

Elizabeth laughed. "Quit pouting, Mr. Darcy. You will not die for lack of a kiss."

"Hmph," was his only response. Letting her go, he held his arm out for her to hold, and after she had done so, he led her to the path where Bingley and Jane waited.

"I say, Darcy, what were you doing back in there? Could you not have spoken to Miss Elizabeth nearer to the path?"

Darcy snorted, "It is not as though you did not wish to be alone with Miss Bennet, Bingley."

Bingley's mouth fell open as both his face and Jane's turned scarlet. Silently, the four of them turned toward the house, arriving just as the bell called them to supper.

After the meal, when the ladies retired to the drawing-room and left the men to their port, Darcy brought up the topic of Wickham to his host.

"Mr. Bennet, I was made aware this evening that a member of the militia has made acquaintance with Elizabeth and her sisters. Normally that would be none of my concern, beyond the part that involves my betrothed, but the officer in question is known to my family and me, and I would be remiss in my duty to yours if I did not warn you about him."

Mr. Bennet's brows had risen during this speech. He was not surprised at his future son-in-law's serious demeanor and usually chose to make sport of him. What did surprise him was that Darcy spoke with such gravity behind his words. Mr. Bennet gestured for him to continue.

"The man, for he does not deserve to be called a gentleman, grew up at Pemberley, the son of my steward." Darcy continued on, repeating the whole sorry story a second time that day, this time keeping out Georgiana's part of it. He had decided while he ate that if he needed to relate that chapter in order to get his betrothed's father to take him seriously he would, but not until then. He rather expected he would need to.

Mr. Bennet reacted to the story exactly as foreseen. He scoffed at the idea that his daughters were in danger.

"They have no dowries to speak of, as you well know, Mr. Darcy. There are women of far greater consequence who will garner this man's attention; he has no need for silly, impoverished girls. No, my daughters are in no danger, though I would be, were I to restrict their movements and their opportunities to speak to and of these militia men. When you have a household full of women, then you will understand, sir."

Bingley spoke up in Darcy's defense, having heard stories at Cambridge about Wickham's exploits, but still Bennet turned a deaf ear. Finally, Darcy held up a hand, stalling Bingley's next words.

"Sir, there is one more offense to be laid at Wickham's door. I had hoped I would not have to share this with you. Bingley knows, of course, as he is my closest friend apart from my cousin. I must ask, though, that it not leave this room. If I hear of it anywhere else, I will know the source." He looked at Mr. Bennet, and seeing he had the man's attention, waited for agreement to his terms.

"Tell me your tale, Mr. Darcy. It will go no further."

Darcy inhaled deeply, then told Mr. Bennet of his sister's near disaster. He finished with, "Mr. Bennet, I have paid for several of Wickham's natural children and their mothers to be placed in service in a town near my estate, or married to strangers. With his propensities to be disrespectful of women and to be wasteful with funds, it would not be difficult to imagine him persuading one of your daughters to become intimate with him, perhaps convince her to run away with him, then steal away in the night with her pin money and leave her ruined. He has, in fact, attempted just such a thing with my own sister. Thankfully, I made an unexpected visit, mere days before they were scheduled to leave, and she admitted the entire scheme to me. I sent Wickham on his way and my recent encounter in Meryton was the first I had seen him since. We did not speak, but I should have known he would learn about my betrothal and try to cause problems."

Mr. Bennet was in shock. He had never considered such a thing, though why he should not have escaped him at the moment. It was not as though he was unaware of the fact that men had relations with women who were not their wives. It was behavior in which he himself had indulged in his years at University, though never with servants or gentlewomen.

"Thank you, Mr. Darcy. You have opened my eyes to the dangers of allowing my daughters to associate too closely with the officers. I

really do not know any of them well
enough, do I? I can assure you, sir,
Mr. Wickham will not be invited
here again, nor will the girls be
permitted to walk into Meryton un-
escorted." He paused as a thought
struck him. "My neighbors. Perhaps a warning in their ears might
not go amiss."

"I believe that to be a sound
idea, though I think it would hold
more weight coming from you."

"Yes, yes, indeed. As a life-
long resident, my word will be taken
as fact immediately. I will visit some
of the neighbors in the morning,
starting with Sir William Lucas. He
is as big a gossip as any female I
have come across. He can assist me
in spreading the word."

"You will not be sorry you
took this step, I promise you."

~~~***~~~

The next day, the militia
found their welcome to the best

188

homes in the area rescinded. What was worse, the town's shopkeepers refused to extend credit and insisted upon payment for what was owed to them. While the majority of the men remained perplexed, two were not. The regiment's commander, Colonel Forster, had received a visit early that morning from Sir William and Mr. Bennet and was given an earful about one of his officers. As a result of that meeting, he increased the number of training exercises his men were required to perform. Had they been welcome to attend dinner parties and balls, they would have been too exhausted to bother.

The other man to be unsurprised at the sudden shunning of he and his colleagues was George Wickham. He was certain Miss Elizabeth had indeed related to Darcy what he had said, and he was equally sure Mr. Darcy had spoken to Mr. Bennet, who took it upon himself to intervene. He did not

Decisions and Consequences

blame Mr. Bennet in the least; he was doing as all good fathers did, he supposed. No, Wickham was angry with Darcy and by extension, Miss Elizabeth Bennet. He vowed revenge on the couple, and sooner rather than later.

Given that maneuvers had increased, Wickham had plenty of time in the next few weeks to think and plan. The more he considered the situation, the more enraged he became, and the more helpless he felt to assuage it. The men under him began to feel that venom directed more and more at them, and they did not like it. They began to mutter and murmur about it, and their unease and unrest began to spread. Finally, it reached Colonel Forster's ears, and he had a word with his newest lieutenant, who he could tell did not appreciate the rebuke.

The good colonel was the least surprised of all the men one morning soon after when Lieutenant

Zoe Burton

Wickham did not show up at the parade grounds for morning formation. The colonel had rather believed, and the men wished, he would remove himself from their company. Of course, desertion from the militia was a serious offense, and should he be caught he would face a firing squad, but he would have to be caught first. Given the situation, Colonel Forster thought it was perhaps best to hold off sending out a search party for him, at least until luncheon.

Chapter 8

The day Elizabeth turned him down, William Collins was at a loss to know what to do with himself. Alternately offended that his suit was summarily dismissed by his cousin, in awe of Mr. Darcy, and worried about returning to Hunsford without the engagement his patroness pressed him to enter, he took himself off for a walk around the park as he dithered about what course to take now.

In the end, it occurred to him that the best approach might be to write Lady Catherine de Bourgh for advice. This he did with alacrity. He sent it to the post and thought some more, mentally reviewing first his remaining cousins and then the other single ladies of the neighborhood.

Decisions and Consequences

His youngest cousin he immediately dismissed as the companion of his future life. She was young and flighty, with high animal spirits. She did not fit his requirements. A minister's wife must be gentle and circumspect, and Miss Lydia was neither. Miss Kitty soon followed her sister in being struck from the list. While he could see the makings of a wife of excellent character in her, she was a lady who followed others, and his spouse needed to be a good example to the wives of his parish. He thought longingly of the eldest Miss Bennet, but he had been warned against her. It was plain to see even for him that Mr. Bingley was besotted with her. Everyone expected him to propose sooner or later, and the young lady's mother insisted he not consider her. That left his middle cousin.

Miss Mary had much to recommend her. She was well-versed in the most popular sermons, as well as Holy Scriptures. She was accomplished on the pianoforte and with a needle. She was, however, a terrible singer. Worse, she had a tendency to preach sermons on every evil she saw. While that was not a bad thing, it would not do for his spouse to be in charge of his parish, and he feared that very thing should he take her to wife. No, Miss Mary would not do, either.

With all of his cousins crossed off his list, Mr. Collins began to contemplate the other ladies in the neighborhood. He made a mental list of arguments for and against each one. In the end, his analysis pointed to Charlotte Lucas being the most likely candidate. She was on the shelf with no immediate prospects and would probably greet his suit with open arms. His mind made up, Mr. Collins made his way to Lucas Lodge, where he was indeed welcomed eagerly.

Decisions and Consequences

Three days later, Miss Lucas made him the happiest of men by accepting his proposal. He promptly moved his belongings to her father's home for the last few days of his visit to Meryton. When he left the following Saturday, he had no idea of the maolotrom that awaited him at home.

Mr. Collins arrived back at Hunsford Parish at exactly four of the clock. He had no more than entered the house when he received a summons from Lady Catherine. As quickly as his legs could carry him, he hastened to her side. The footman escorted him to the drawing room, announced him, and exited, closing the clergyman in with his angry patroness.

"Mr. Collins," the great lady boomed. "What is the meaning of the letter I received from you just three days ago?"

Nervously, Collins cleared his throat. "My lady, I am sorry to disappoint you by not returning betrothed to one of my cousins, but I assure you I am engaged. To a-"

"I am not concerned about that. Do you mean to tell me that my nephew, Mr. Darcy, has engaged himself to one of your inferior cousins?" Lady Catherine's eyes were narrowed and her face red, so red that Mr. Collins worried for her health.

"Y-y-yes, h-h-h-he d-d-did." He nervously played with the buttons on his tailcoat. "W-w-with." He swallowed. "M-m—Miss E-Elizabeth."

"Miss Elizabeth Bennet." It sounded almost like a question, but not quite. Mr. Collins just bobbed his head in response, not certain an actual answer was required—or desired.

"A Miss Elizabeth Bennet thinks she is engaged to my daughter's betrothed? It cannot be. It will not stand! Why did you not speak to him about this abomination?"

Suddenly Mr. Collins came to the horrified realization that Mr. Darcy was already engaged, or so

Decisions and Consequences

Lady Catherine insisted, to Miss Anne de Bourgh, her daughter. His nerves, overset by the unexpected onslaught of Lady Catherine's anger, set his lips to moving with an amazing speed.

"I am so sorry, Lady Catherine. I did not know that Mr. Darcy was Miss De Bourgh's betrothed, or I would have done everything in my power to separate him from my unworthy cousin. I know he would have listened to me and agreed to end his association-"

"Enough! You have failed me in this, and I shall not forget it. I will take care of the problem myself. Go back to the parsonage. I will call you when I require your presence again."

Bowing repeatedly, the clergyman backed to the door and then, after fumbling behind him for the handle, out into the hall. He wiped the sweat from his brow with his handkerchief as he scurried back to the parsonage. He was happy to get out of Rosings still in possession of his living.

Back at Rosings, Lady Catherine De Bourgh was pacing the drawing room, fuming. Her anger ebbed and flowed, first against her nephew for defying her wishes and those of his dearly departed mother, and then against this Miss Elizabeth Bennet, who dared steal another's betrothed and the young woman's parents, who obviously raised her to be a grasping social climber.

For a brief moment, as she thought of her deceased sister, Lady Anne Fitzwilliam Darcy, she had a twinge of conscience. The two ladies had been complete opposites. Catherine was aggressive and bold, even as a girl. Anne was mild-mannered and sweet. As the daughters of an earl, both were used to getting their own way, but they went about getting it differently. Lady Anne was not a pushover, though. She was more than capable of holding her ground against anyone, including her dominant older sister. Many times, while their children were young, had they butted heads. Catherine had pushed from the moment her daughter, Anne, was born to engage her to Lady Anne's son, Fitzwilliam. Lady Anne Darcy, with the support of her husband, George, had refused. She insisted her son was too young for his future to be so decided, and that she would never consent to such an archaic practice. She desired that he marry where he would, as she and her George had.

Lady Catherine strenuously argued her point every time they were together, but Lady Anne never relented. When her only sister died twelve years later, Catherine began pushing her brother-in-law to agree. As grief-stricken as he was, at first, he ignored her. Over the course of time, as his grief dulled and his emotions became better able to handle her, he maintained his dead wife's position on the matter. Fitzwilliam would marry where he wished, with no interference from anyone. He went so far as to forbid Lady Catherine to speak of it in his presence and that of his son, and then spoke to the earl himself. When her brother, who had come into his title just a year before Lady Anne's death, insisted she desist, Catherine indignantly retreated to Rosings. She only began speaking of it again following George Darcy's death five years previously. Unknown to her, however, her nephew had been informed long before his father's death that his aunt was likely to insist he marry his cousin and that he was in no way obligated to do so. It was merely a wish of Lady Catherine's and had no bearing on reality. As a result, young Darcy never responded to her when she spoke of it. He simply ignored her. Lady Catherine mistakenly took this for complaisance. She now regretted doing so.

Well, no more, she thought. *I now know the treachery Darcy is capable of. I must plan a strategy: find a way to work on the lady and her family.* She was certain her nephew would not listen to reason, convinced as she was that he had deceived her. She spent the rest of the evening and most of the next day planning. On Monday morning, she began to put the pieces in place, first writing to her solicitor to attend her, and then calling her rector to come to Rosings so she could grill him about the estate he would inherit and its inhabitants. In the end, it would be almost a fortnight before she acted. When she did, it would have repercussions that she did not anticipate.

Lady Catherine arrived in Meryton six days prior to Christmas. Her arrival in a coach and six, unexpected as it was, caused quite a stir. Speculation about the occupants of the vehicle ran rampant until it turned off the main road and into the lane for Lucas Lodge. The townspeople realized then that it must be Mr. Collins' patroness, or, at least, her equipage dropping him off to see his betrothed. Everyone went back about their business, but with one eye to the road, wanting to know if Lady Catherine had accompanied her rector and if so, what she looked like. One family in the area would soon have intimate knowledge of her looks, as well as her reasons for coming.

After leaving Mr. Collins at Lucas Lodge, the great lady's coach turned toward Longbourn. Her first plan of attack was to speak to the insignificant chit who presumed to marry higher than she should.

Alighting from the carriage, Lady Catherine looked about, taking in the elegant house and grounds. She was surprised at how well-maintained it was. When her rector had told her of the small dowries of the daughters of the house, she had assumed the family was in dire straits. She had planned to use that as leverage and offer a sum of money in exchange for the engagement being broken. It appeared she may need to revise that strategy somewhat.

Upon being admitted to the building, she followed the servant to a west-facing drawing room. The thought crossed her mind that it must be a terribly uncomfortable room in the summer, what with the large, floor-to-ceiling windows. *I must instruct this woman to use another room in the summer.*

She nodded to the group of women gathered in the room to acknowledge their curtseys and then began to speak. "I am looking for Miss Elizabeth Bennet. I wish to speak to her immediately and in private."

Mrs. Bennet was a little in awe of her newest guest, whom she knew from Mr. Darcy to be his aunt. She gestured to her second daughter. "This is Elizabeth, my lady. And next to her is-"

"I do not need any further introductions. I will speak to Miss Elizabeth alone." Lady Catherine looked down her nose at Mrs. Bennet with a haughty air that declared her consequence, not to mention her temperament, to the world.

"Come, girls, to the kitchen." She began to herd her other children out of the room. She wondered what the lady wanted with Elizabeth but was not about to ask.

When the door closed behind them, Lady Catherine turned to see that Elizabeth was looking at her with an unreadable expression. Unable to stare her down, Mr. Darcy's aunt instead used every argument she had in her formidable arsenal to try to convince the young woman to give up her engagement.

"It can be no surprise to you, Miss Bennet, why I have come here."

"No, it is not. Mr Darcy told me of you and warned me what you were like. I am not at all surprised that you came, nor am I in wonder as to the reason." Elizabeth silently considered informing Lady Catherine straight away that she would not break the engagement, for she was certain that was the lady's purpose, but decided that would be impertinent and that it was better to maintain her hold on propriety and be respectful.

"Then you will understand me when I say this engagement must be broken off immediately."

"I am very much afraid, Lady Catherine, that it is impossible to do so."

"Impossible? Nothing is impossible! Think, if you will, of your upbringing. You were not raised to the society that Darcy inhabits. You will be ridiculed and scorned; you will never be accepted."

Elizabeth was mildly amused with the pomposity with which this statement was put forth and it showed in the small smirk on her face. "How well do you know your nephew, madam? Even I, who have been acquainted with him for mere weeks, am aware that he does nothing without careful deliberation. Therefore, he has already considered such an occurrence and dismissed it as of no importance. He has assured me that we will continue his habit of attending select events held by those with whom he has a good relationship and who will not question his choice of a wife. I am not afraid. And, if he is not concerned, why should you be?"

Lady Catherine's anger became greater. "He is engaged to my daughter!" she thundered. "What have you to say to that? Would you have him break her heart and ruin her future?"

"If it were true that he was engaged to Miss de Bourgh he would not have made an offer to me. He is an honorable man; to betroth himself to one woman while promised to another would be counter to every ideal he holds dear. Truly, Lady Catherine, I cannot, nay, I will not, break this engagement. You had better return to your home and comfort your daughter, if indeed she requires it, and leave off railing at me."

That statement would be the last Elizabeth would add to the conversation. It angered Lady Catherine greatly. Added to this, every time Elizabeth insisted it would be impossible for her to end her engagement, Lady Catherine's rage grew; along with it rose the volume of her voice. She had just thrown the term "fortune hunter" at the ungrateful chit when the door was thrown open, slamming it back against the wall and a voice she knew well roared, "Enough!"

Elizabeth, who had begun to wonder how it was that no one in the entire household could hear this woman attack her and what exactly the use was of a gentleman who could not or would not save her from such a thing, his aunt or not, was greatly relieved.

Darcy planted himself between his betrothed and his mother's sister. Keeping his eyes on Lady Catherine, he reached back for Elizabeth's hand. Once she placed it in his grasp, he squeezed it, stating, "I apologize for my aunt. Are you well?"

Taking a deep breath, she replied, "As well as can be expected, considering the circumstances. I had begun to think I would never be rescued and would have to call for Mr. Hill to remove her."

"I did not realize she was here. We were in the back of the bookroom when she pulled in and could not see from our vantage point whose coach it was. I just now heard her begin to berate you. Why do you not go to your father and wait with him while I take care of this?" He glanced at her quickly, willing her to do as he asked.

"Very well, I shall." She turned to Lady Catherine and curtseyed. "Good day. I trust that the next time we meet, it will be under better circumstances."

Darcy's aunt did not deign to respond. Darcy noticed, and stayed his betrothed's departure until she did. Once Elizabeth left the room, he began speaking.

"You were not expected, Aunt. I wonder at your coming so far, un-invited."

"You know very well why I am here. You are betrothed to *my daughter.* I could not let this farce of an engagement continue one day longer while she sits at home with a broken heart."

210

Darcy scoffed. "I seriously doubt Anne is broken-hearted. I would not be at all surprised to hear she is even now inviting the neighborhood for a grand celebration."

"How could you say such a thing? You have been engaged since your infancy. Of course her heart is broken!"

"We have not been engaged since our infancy. That is your desire. Not hers, not mine, not my father's nor my mother's. Yours, and yours alone. Anne has never desired a match with me, nor I, her. I chose to leave you to your speculation, as did she, but we have discussed it every year for as long as I can remember, and we are in agreement that you would simply have to bear the disappointment."

"B-bear the disappointment? You were formed for each other..."

"Enough, Aunt! I will not hear another word about it. I am engaged to Miss Elizabeth Bennet. I chose her above all others I have met. She will be the perfect wife and Mistress. She handled you magnificently, and I am certain had I not been here, she would have tossed you out on your ear as you so richly deserve. Elizabeth does not suffer fools gladly, and you, Aunt Catherine, are a fool. You will apologize to her, to her family, and to me."

"We can break-"

"No," he roared. "I will marry her and no other. Do you understand me?"

Her lips tightened into a thin line before she nodded.

A thought came to Darcy. "Is the earl aware you are here?" When his aunt's face turned white, he got his answer. "He is not, I see. Well, perhaps I will share this little bit of information with him. You know how he hates it when someone connected to Matlock tarnishes the name. This poorly executed trip of yours certainly qualifies as that."

212

"No, Darcy." She swallowed, hating what she would have to do next. "I beg you not to tell him. I have no desire for him to poke his nose into my business."

Darcy eyed her speculatively. He had felt for years that her meddling in the affairs of others was out of control and that she needed a firm hand to keep her in check. "No," he replied slowly, "I believe it to be the right thing to do. I will, however, ask him to be merciful. There is only so much he can do to you, after all. But you require someone else to review your books every year, since I am marrying. Then, too, until you apologize to my betrothed and her family, you will be cut off from the Darcys, making it impossible for me to continue doing so. Now then, I must ask you to leave. Please be kind to Mr. Hill on your way out." He bowed to his aunt, turning on his heel and leaving the room.

Decisions and Consequences

Lady Catherine stood silently for a minute, unable to take in what had transpired and what Darcy's parting words had been. Silently, she followed the servant out, climbed into the coach, and rode away.

In the house, Darcy was entering Mr. Bennet's bookroom to assure himself of Elizabeth's well-being. He found her sitting beside her father on a chaise by the desk. Mr. Bennet was holding her hand, looking bemused. His betrothed wore a stoic look, but he could see traces of anger in her eyes. He knelt beside her, reaching to take her free hand in his own.

"Are you well, Elizabeth?"

"I am. That, I take it, was your aunt?"

"Yes, unfortunately."

"The same aunt who wanted you to marry her daughter?" Darcy had explained the situation to her on one of their walks recently, when she had asked about his extended family.

"Yes."

"Apparently, we both have relations who cause us great embarrassment," she stated tartly.

Despite the seriousness of the situation, Darcy chuckled. "Indeed, we do."

"And am I expected to entertain that harridan even as I am supposed to keep my mother at a distance?"

The words sobered Darcy immediately. To his shame, he realized the unfairness of separating her from her family while requiring her to deal with the ridiculous members of his. He looked down, his cheeks aflame. "No," he began softly. "I cannot ask it of you. I am sorry I ever entertained the notion."

The tightness around Elizabeth's eyes and mouth eased somewhat. "Very well. I am sorry for behaving badly just now."

Mr. Bennet, who was amused at the manner in which his favorite daughter set down the man she was soon to marry, rose and walked behind the desk to take a seat. He was enjoying this, yet he wished to be far enough away that he was not in the way of any objects that might be thrown or otherwise damaged, should Mr. Darcy put his foot in his mouth again. One did not live in a houseful of women for three and twenty years without learning to get out of the way when there was an argument. His caution was unnecessary, for seeing the shame in her betrothed's face, Elizabeth relented and forgave him.

Chapter 9

To the relief of everyone in the Bennet household, the Christmas holiday passed with no more visits from angry relatives. Instead, there were holiday parties and engagement dinners, and another ball at Netherfield.

It was at this ball that Charles Bingley finally gathered the courage to propose to Jane. He had taken his friend's words to heart and had examined his sisters' words and actions more closely. He had also paid keen attention to Jane, and to his joy, saw that she did indeed treat those she cared about with a little more tenderness and that she extended it to him. When Darcy proposed a quick, overnight trip to London to shop for his sister and Elizabeth, Bingley jumped at the opportunity. While in town, he bought a beautiful sapphire and diamond ring for Jane, and bracelets for his sisters. He spent his time in the carriage planning where he would propose and what he would say. He had not been so eager for anything since he was a boy.

Darcy also bought jewelry, for while Elizabeth would wear his mother's wedding ring and have access to all the family jewels, he wanted her to have something all her own. He chose a set consisting of a necklace, bracelet, and earbobs. The stones were emeralds surrounded by diamonds. They would, he knew, be set off beautifully against her dark hair and creamy skin.

He was eager to present them to her. He knew she might be uncomfortable, and he further knew his gift, assuming he got one, would likely be something she made or bought in Meryton. That did not matter to him. It was important that she begin married life with as many advantages as possible. He had not a doubt in the world of her ability to hold her own, but a little help now and then would not be remiss.

The pair arrived back in Meryton the evening before the ball. They visited Longbourn for an hour or two in the morning, then returned to Netherfield to prepare for the festivities.

When the Bennet family arrived that evening, Darcy was standing at a window, watching for them. Though the courtyard was well-lit by the numerous flaming torches around the perimeter, it was difficult to make out who was whom as they exited their carriage. All the ladies were bundled against the cold of the night with hooded capes that kept him from seeing their faces. Suddenly, as though sensing she was being watched, one of them lifted her face to the row of windows. It was Elizabeth. His breath stuck in his throat as his eyes caught hers and held. He lifted his hand to wave. When she returned the gesture, he turned from the window to hasten to greet her. The rational, logical part of his mind wondered at his reaction, but the reckless, irrational part of him that he usually kept under strict regulation pushed those thoughts back, determined to enjoy this evening with the woman who, in less than a week, would be joined to him forever.

Arriving at the bottom of the staircase, Darcy stopped and waited for Elizabeth and her sisters to remove their cloaks, straighten their hair, and exchange their shoes for dancing slippers. He greeted each one with a bow and a murmured, "Good evening." Finally, Jane and Elizabeth exited the room. Darcy bowed to their curtseys, then straightened and offered his arm for his betrothed to hold. She did so, slipping her hand into the crook of his elbow.

"You look lovely this evening, Elizabeth."

Her brow arched, she looked up at him. "Handsome enough to tempt you, then?"

Darcy groaned. "Will I ever live that down?"

"Oh, I very much doubt it." Elizabeth's laugh as the pair took their places in the receiving line caused every eye to look their way. Darcy shook his head. *Teasing wench,* he thought.

Thirty minutes later, after having greeted what felt like the majority of the population of Meryton and half of London, he leaned down to whisper in Elizabeth's ear, "Tell me again why we are part of the receiving line?"

"We are the engaged couple. Everyone wishes to see us."

"And they cannot do that in the ballroom?"

Decisions and Consequences

Elizabeth turned, hands on hips, and whispered furiously, "Mr. Darcy, are you whining?"

With a pout and a sniff, he raised his nose and responded, "No. A Darcy never whines. I merely asked a question."

Rolling her eyes, Elizabeth did not answer him. Instead, she turned back to the next guest waiting to greet her. Fitzwilliam would just have to suffer.

Finally, the last of the guests arrived and the hosts and guests of honor entered the ballroom. Darcy led his soon-to-be-wife to a group of people standing to the side of the room. One was a young blonde girl, about Lydia's age, one was a soldier, and the other two members of the group were older.

Darcy bowed to the elder couple. "Uncle, Aunt, it is good to see you this evening."

"You as well, Nephew. Your aunt and I could not let you marry without some of your family in attendance. I know Lady Catherine was here to cause trouble. I did not want you to think we are minded as she is."

"Thank you, sir."

Lord Matlock cleared his throat. "Well, then. Is this lovely lady your bride?"

"Yes, she is! Lord Matlock, Lady Matlock, this is Miss Elizabeth Bennet. Elizabeth, this is my aunt and uncle."

"We are pleased to make your acquaintance," Lord Matlock stated. "We had begun to despair of Darcy ever marrying. I apologize on behalf of my sister. She had no business accosting you."

Lady Matlock added, "Yes, we are so very pleased! You are a lovely young lady, and from what Darcy has told us in his letters, you are quite accomplished. We must get together before the wedding and have a chat. I have long stood in for his poor mother, and I am certain I can give you some advice on how to handle him." She winked at Elizabeth as the entire group burst into chuckles.

"I will, Lady Matlock, I thank you. I am certain I will need all the help I can get. And thank you, Lord Matlock, for your apology. I must say I am delighted that you are so welcoming."

"My sister can be...overwhelming. I am told you stood up to her quite bravely. She does not like that, but she will respect you all the more for it."

Darcy next introduced his betrothed to the soldier and the girl.

"Colonel Richard Fitzwilliam, Miss Georgiana Darcy, this is Miss Elizabeth Bennet. Elizabeth, this is my cousin and my sister."

Georgiana was trembling with both excitement and fear at meeting her new sister. She hoped with all her heart they would be friends, and when she greeted Elizabeth, she haltingly told her so. She was greatly relieved when her brother's betrothed warmly held her hands and smiled, assuring her that she was looking forward to adding to her number of siblings. When Elizabeth went so far as to tease about borrowed gowns and ribbons, Georgiana's smile was bright enough to light the entire room.

As was all his family, Darcy was delighted to see this sign of healing in Georgiana. It seemed that her ragged emotions were finally leveling off, and his instincts that she needed a sister were correct. It was a relief to do something right for her after failing so miserably this past summer.

Colonel Fitzwilliam took advantage of a break in the conversation to ask a question of his cousin's betrothed. "Miss Elizabeth, I noticed that you arrived with several young ladies. Were those your sisters?" He had noticed one of the young ladies seemed uneasy, and he wondered why someone so pretty would feel that way. It was a mystery, and he was intrigued.

"Yes, Colonel, they were. There are five of us. My eldest sister, Jane, is there behind you, with Mr. Bingley."

The colonel turned and was relieved to see that this sister was not the one who so interested him.

Elizabeth looked around the room, finally spotting Kitty and Lydia laughing with Maria Lucas at the edge of the dancing area and Mary just sitting down beside her mother. "My two youngest sisters are there," she pointed to them, "with a young girl in pale green. They are Kitty and Lydia, and their friend is Maria Lucas."

Richard nodded. "Yes, I believe Sir William introduced her to me when we arrived. You have one more sister?"

Elizabeth smiled. "Yes, along the first row of chairs, just this way of the column, you will see my mother gesticulating as she speaks. My sister Mary is seated to the left of her. She is the one with the book."

"Ah, I see her. Might I ask for an introduction to her?"

Elizabeth's brows rose almost to her hairline. She looked at the colonel for a couple of moments, as though trying to discern his intent. Deciding to trust him after looking to Mr. Darcy and seeing his nod, she agreed and led the men to her quietest sister.

"Mary," she began. Her sister looked up in surprise. It was rare anyone spoke to her at the beginning of a ball. They were usually too busy finding partners for the first sets. "Mary, there is someone here who would like to meet you."

Mary rose, covering her shock as best she could.

Decisions and Consequences

"Colonel Fitzwilliam, this is my next sister, Miss Mary Bennet. Mary, this is Mr. Darcy's cousin, Colonel Richard Fitzwilliam."

Richard bowed. "How do you do, Miss Mary?"

Mary curtseyed. "I am well, thank you, Colonel. I am pleased to meet you."

"I was wondering if you were engaged for all the dances?"

Now Mary's astonishment could not be concealed. No one ever asked her to dance before, not until they were well into their cups. She stumbled over her answer. "I-I am not."

"Then, would you honor me with your hand for a set?"

Mary swallowed, her mouth dry. "Certainly, sir."

Richard was amused by her shy responses. He felt protective of her, which was unusual for him, especially for someone he had just met.

"May I have the supper set?"

228

"Yes, sir, you may."

"Thank you, Miss Mary. I shall leave you to your book and return in plenty of time for our dance." Bowing, he smiled at her, grinned at his cousin, and walked away.

The musicians just then began to play

"Come, Elizabeth, we are leading the first set."

"Of course."

Nodding to Mary as Elizabeth once again hooked her hand over his arm, Darcy proudly led her to the head of the line of dancers. Taking his place opposite, he called over to her, "Thank you for putting Georgiana at ease. She has been anxious about meeting you, and your feelings about her misstep last summer."

By now the dance had begun, and his last words were spoken quietly enough that only Elizabeth could hear. He himself had explained Georgiana's situation to her

Decisions and Consequences

on one of their walks. Upon hearing the tale, Elizabeth's anger at Wickham, and her relief in asking Darcy about him, was great. Darcy was sure that had she been a man, she would have immediately called Wickham out. He was beginning to understand Mr Bennet's penchant for hiding in his bookroom. Female emotions apparently ran strong. He could only imagine what it would be like to be stuck in the house with six of them at once. Realizing there would be at least two in his own home after his honeymoon, he shivered, struck by a sudden vision of thrown knickknacks and red-faced, screaming women. He shook his head to clear that vision from his mind. He refused to fear. He was certain Elizabeth would never behave in that manner.

As he and his betrothed moved down the dance, they continued to converse, sometimes on serious topics and other times on lighter ones. Darcy was struck with how at ease they had become with each other. They were now ten days from the wedding. They had spent four weeks in each other's company as often as possible, and he could say now with certainty that he quite liked Elizabeth.

For her part, Elizabeth was beginning to realize the same thing. The man she had thought haughty and controlling had a softer side. She had known from the start that he was intelligent, but she had learned that he was a good and liberal master, with a generous heart. She was starting to feel as though they might get on very well together. He did have some rough edges, to be sure. There were aspects to him that she could not like. Perhaps, however, her presence in his life might soften them. He may learn from her example to be as generous and kind to those without his circle as he was those within. Elizabeth was satisfied that she had made the best choice for her future.

Darcy had asked Elizabeth to reserve for him three sets: the first, the supper, and the last set. This was the maximum number of dances allowed for any couple, and despite the enjoyment each felt at having such an accomplished partner, they were forced to dance with others in between.

They left the dance floor following the first set, both thirsty after the vigorous dance. As they passed by Mrs. Bennet, they heard her in conversation with one of the neighbors.

"How graceful they are together! It is as though they were formed for each other. How proud you must be, Mrs. Bennet."

"Oh, indeed. Very proud. Though I must say, I cannot think what would have attracted Mr. Darcy to Lizzy. She has nothing much to recommend her. She is not beautiful like Jane, nor is she lively like my Lydia."

As her mother's words faded away, Elizabeth tried to ignore the little bit of hurt they caused. She had stiffened without realizing it, and when Darcy laid his free hand over hers that lay on his arm, she glanced at him. He was looking at her with concern etched into his features.

"Are you well, Elizabeth?"

She nodded. "Yes, quite well. I am not a stranger to my mother's opinions of me."

"You are hurt by them, though. I can see it in your face."

"Yes," she confessed, "I am, though I ought not to be, I know. I had rather hoped my betrothal would put a stop to her comments...that I might finally be acceptable to her, but it seems that I still lack something."

"I would not have you put any stock in what she says. I chose you for reasons you already know, and as I have come to know you further, I am increasingly certain that my decision was the correct one. You are perfect as my betrothed and you will be perfect as Mrs Darcy. There is nothing I would have you change."

"Thank you, Fitzwilliam. I will do my best to ensure that your faith in me is not misplaced."

"It could never be," he assured her. "I must confess that your mother's words have angered me, Elizabeth. I have half a mind to tell her so. I fear, however, she would deny saying anything negative about you. I suspect she does not realize what she is saying."

"She does not. Jane and I, and Papa, have tried to explain to her in the past how her words affect others and how she sounds when she says things, but she does not understand. I know she loves me, but I am more like my father than any of my sisters. She does not understand Papa and she does not understand me." She shrugged. "Apparently, she does not understand you, either, since she cannot grasp your reasons for wanting to marry me." Elizabeth rolled her eyes as she finished speaking, eliciting a chuckle from Darcy.

"I will keep my thoughts to myself tonight." They laughed again before he continued in all seriousness, "I would have her understand that I will not tolerate disrespect to my wife from anyone, including her mother. I will persist with it until she ceases her demeaning comments."

"Thank you, Fitzwilliam. I wish you the best of luck." She winked at him and he squeezed her hand in return.

After retrieving glasses of punch from the servant who was pouring out, the pair wandered to the other side of the room, away from Elizabeth's mother, and found seats near her sister, Mary. They began discussing the book Mary had brought, as it was one they both had previously read. They tried to draw Mary into the conversation, asking her opinion of what she had read so far, and if she was looking forward to her dance with the colonel. Mary was a studious girl and shy. She hated balls, preferring to read or play the pianoforte. She was a little intimidated by her sister's betrothed, but she soaked in the attention they gave her, for she rarely received anyone's undivided attention unless she was performing.

Soon, Bingley and Jane joined them. Bingley requested dances from both Elizabeth and a surprised Mary. Darcy did likewise, asking Jane for the next dance and Mary for her next available set. Mary was astonished to be asked to dance so much, her sisters, Bingley, and Darcy, less so. As Elizabeth and Darcy informed her later, she was soon to be part of the Darcy extended family, and that connection was a highly prized one. Her consequence would be raised significantly upon their marriage, and she must come to expect more attention.

"As a matter of fact, Mary, I would love for you to join us for a season. Mr. Darcy's sister is coming out in a year or two. It would give us good practice for her if you would allow us to sponsor you." Turning to Darcy, she exclaimed, "Oh! I am sorry, I should have consulted you before I made the offer."

"No, no, it is fine. I like your idea." Darcy had come to realize in the last few weeks that this sister was largely ignored, and this evening's discussion had shown him that, given the proper kind of attention, she had the potential to turn out much as Elizabeth had. "I should be delighted to host you, Miss Mary. Please, say you will allow us to do this for you."

Decisions and Consequences

Mary blushed in a mixture of surprise and pleasure. No one had ever requested her presence in such a manner before, and she found she rather liked it. "Thank you, Mr Darcy, Lizzy I I believe I shall, as long as Papa approves."

Elizabeth took her sister's hand and squeezed it. "Oh, I am sure he will. And if he does not, I will work to convince him."

"Thank you, Lizzy," Mary exclaimed. It was all she could do to maintain proper behavior and not squeal like Lydia would do. Try as she might, though, she could not remove the wide smile from her face. Her interest in the book she brought waned to the point of non-existence.

By the end of the night, the Bennet girls had danced almost every dance, including one each with Colonel Fitzwilliam and Lord Matlock. The behavior of the youngest two was a shock to those two men, who wondered how Mr. Bennet could allow them out when they clearly did not understand proper behavior and how he could have raised two superior daughters and yet have two more who ran wild.

Colonel Fitzwilliam was particularly taken with two of the eldest Bennet girls. Jane Bennet was one of the most beautiful ladies he had ever seen. He could see that she and Bingley were lost in each other, and knew he could not come between them and remain an honorable gentleman, so with regret, he turned his thoughts away from her.

The other sister who intrigued him was Miss Mary. She was very quiet during their dance, and he noticed in her a tendency to preach proper behavior when she did speak, but he saw a certain strength in her that he liked very much. He did his best both during their dance and at supper to draw her out, and realized that his attention caused her to blossom a bit, similarly to

Decisions and Consequences

what he had witnessed when she danced with his cousin and his father. He knew from their conversation that she would be having a Season with Darcy and his new wife. He determined he would keep an eye on her and see what she made of herself with this opportunity. He could bide his time to be sure she was what he wanted in a wife, and if she fell in love with someone else in that time, he would know it was not meant to be and move on.

That night, in the middle of the ballroom, at the end of the supper set and before they went to the dining room, Bingley dropped to his knee and begged his Jane to be his wife. When she tearfully, happily, consented, the room erupted in applause loud enough to drown out Mrs. Bennet's effusions. The remainder of the ball passed in a happy haze for Bingley and Jane.

At the end of the night, the Bennets were the last to leave.

Though exhausted, Mrs. Bennet still could not control her joy at her eldest daughter's conquest. "Two daughters married!" rang out from the Bennet carriage more than once as it drove away.

Darcy and his family all ascended the staircase together. Georgiana had retired hours before, as she was not out and not permitted to attend the majority of the ball. She had sat beside her aunt until supper, when she went to her rooms to eat with her companion and go to bed.

"Well, Darcy, that is quite a family you are marrying into."

"Yes, Uncle, it is. There are some members of the family who leave something to be desired," he exchanged glances with Lord Matlock, "but then, after Lady Catherine's visit, I can hardly claim superiority in that area."

"Indeed."

"I quite like your betrothed," Lady Matlock quietly stated. "As a matter of fact, I adore her. She reminds me so much of our Adele." The Matlocks had lost a daughter to childbirth eighteen months ago and had not been long out of mourning for her. The loss was still keenly felt, and the lady needed to pause a moment before she could finish speaking. "Miss Elizabeth is a strong-minded young lady. I quite enjoyed our conversation at supper tonight. You have done well, Fitzwilliam. Your parents would be proud of you."

"Yes," Lord Matlock added his agreement, "they would. Very proud." He clapped his nephew on the shoulder as they reached Darcy's rooms. "She is delightful, and I am beyond happy to welcome her to the family, and make it clear to society that she is one of us. Do not fear what your aunt has told you, or Miss Elizabeth. I will keep Catherine in check."

"Thank you, sir. She said the same about the two of you. We appreciate your support."

The party wished each other a good night then, each heading to their own rooms.

Chapter 10

The Gardiners stayed on at Longbourn for more time than was their custom, in order to be in attendance at Elizabeth's wedding. They came to know and appreciate Mr. Darcy, and he, them. He extended an invitation for them to stay at Pemberley in the coming summer when they took their planned trip to the Lakes. Elizabeth's appreciation for the gesture made to her favorite people in the world was manifested later that day during their walk, in a kiss that left him breathless and shaking with desire.

Lord and Lady Matlock also stayed in the area, at Netherfield, for the next few days, to represent Darcy's family at the wedding. Colonel Fitzwilliam was required to return to London to attend his duties, but was scheduled to return the day before the wedding.

While the Matlocks appreciated Bingley's hospitality in hosting them for the duration of their stay, their gratitude was tempered by his sisters, especially the youngest of the two.

Caroline Bingley had been mortified to learn of Darcy's betrothal to Miss Elizabeth. She could not understand his reasons for choosing someone not of the first circles. She herself had all the qualities a gentleman was supposed to be looking for. She was educated at a leading seminary for young ladies, where she learned all the proper topics: etiquette, embroidery, painting, and languages. She knew how to plan an event, how to direct servants and manage a household, and how to mingle with those of superior rank. She was accepted into all the best homes and had tickets at Almack's. She knew who was related

to whom and who was acceptable
company for someone of her status.
Miss Elizabeth knew none of this.
She had never been to school. She
was far from the model of propriety.
The woman walked the countryside
alone, for heaven's sake! And the
reading...it ooomed all Miss Elizabeth enjoyed was reading. She did
not play cards the entire time she
was at Netherfield, nor did she do
much needlework. It never occurred
to Miss Bingley that Elizabeth's
maid had simply not packed her
embroidery in with her clothes for
her brief stay.

Miss Bingley had done her
best to talk Mr. Darcy out of what
she saw as a disastrous alignment
between himself and the Bennets.
They had relatives in trade, she argued. Mrs. Bennet and the younger
girls were ridiculous, she com-
plained. His standing in society
would be damaged, she warned.
Nothing worked. Every argument

she put forth was soundly rejected. When she began to question his sanity in offering for such an inferior creature to herself, he turned icily cold, informing her that his standing was none of her concern. She was, to her mind, understandably upset by his stance. However, with his aunt and uncle in the house, she felt she had one more chance to persuade him. She did not wait long to gain an audience with them, tracking them down the day after the ball, relaxing in a sitting room.

Miss Bingley entered the room, shutting the doors behind her. Curtseying to the couple, she greeted them.

"Good afternoon, Lord Matlock, Lady Matlock."

"Miss Bingley," Lady Matlock replied while her husband nodded. "Thank you for your kind invitation to stay with you. This is a beautiful house."

"Thank you, my lady." She paused, suddenly nervous about what she was about to say. "I was hoping I could have a moment of your time," she tentatively requested.

Lady Matlock raised her eyebrows. She could not imagine what this young lady would want with them, but as she supposed it could not hurt to give her an audience, she nodded her permission.

Caroline took a deep breath and then began, "I wished for you to know that I have done my best to dissuade Mr. Darcy from this imprudent marriage, but have failed utterly. I have pointed out to him all the pitfalls of such a relationship, but he has soundly rejected each of my arguments. He seems uncaring that his reputation will be sullied and that he will be seen as a laughingstock. Now that you are here," she continued earnestly, "perhaps you can succeed where I have failed."

Decisions and Consequences

"Miss-," Lord Matlock ceased speaking when he saw his wife lift her hand to stop him.

"Miss Bingley," Lady Matlock began, "how can you be so sure he will be censured by society, or that we ourselves look down on his choice?"

This took Miss Bingley a little by surprise. "Why, Miss Elizabeth has relatives in trade! Her uncle is the solicitor in this worthless excuse for a town, and she has another who lives in Cheapside! Her accomplishments are few, and she is practically poverty-stricken!" A sudden, horrifying, thought struck her. "Surely you do not condone this marriage?"

"Indeed, we do. Let me address your concerns and you will see why. To begin with, Miss Elizabeth is far from poor. Yes, her portion is small, but her father is a landed gentleman. They have servants aplenty...enough to see to their needs, at least. They keep a carriage and horses. They wear fine clothing. Certainly not the most expensive fabrics, but very fine. Again I say, the Bennet family is far from poor.

"As for her relatives being in trade, did you not meet them last evening? One would not know they were not gentry, to meet them on the street. They could easily be mistaken for people of fashion. Mr. Gardiner must, I think, do very well for himself." Lady Matlock looked to her husband. "My dear, did he not say he lived in Gracechurch Street, *near* Cheapside?"

Lord Matlock, now attuned to what his wife was doing, nodded. "Yes, that is what he said. He is within sight of his warehouses, but is not within the Cheapside district."

Caroline was stunned at what she was hearing. She simply could not believe they wished their nephew to marry beneath himself.

Lady Matlock took up her cause once again. "As for accomplishments, why, I believe she speaks at least two languages fluently. When I spoke to her last evening, she seemed well-read and intelligent. She was able to converse on a wider array of topics than is usually found in a young lady of her age. And, when she took her turn playing for us at supper, I thought her performance everything charming. Do you not agree, Henry?"

"I do! Certainly, she was not perfect. She missed a note here and there, but her playing was so...unaffected...she allowed her emotions to infuse the piece and that quite negated any negative effect of missing notes."

Lady Matlock smiled at her husband. He was very fond of music, though he rarely let on he was. She turned back to Miss Bingley.

"I know that she has been trained to run a household, as well. Best of all, she has the courage to look forward to the challenge that running my nephew's properties will entail. She is not flighty, as so many young ladies are nowadays. And what is most important to Darcy is that she is honest. I can attest to that myself. All in all, Miss Bingley, I must admit that I greatly admire Miss Elizabeth and am eager to have her take her place in the family. I have already told my nephew, and I will share with you now, that she very much reminds me of the daughter I lost not long ago. Miss Elizabeth will never replace my girl, but I," Lady Matlock looked to her husband, "both of us, welcome her with open arms."

"But-."

The Matlocks rose. "Good day, Miss Bingley. I hope that you will desist in this obvious attempt to ruin Darcy's happiness. He is pleased with his choice, and as we love him like our own son, we support him. He will be welcomed by society, as will his wife, I can guarantee it." The powerful couple turned as one and exited the room, leaving Caroline staring after them in disbelief.

Despite their clear words to her, Miss Bingley persisted in disbelieving that they could desire Elizabeth Bennet as their niece. Every time she saw an opportunity to persuade them, she took it. Lord and Lady Matlock began spending nearly as much time at Longbourn as Darcy did.

Finally, the wedding day arrived, sunny, cold, and bright. Elizabeth woke early, as was her wont. She chose, however, to dispense with her usual morning walk. Instead, she settled into the window seat and watched the estate begin to stir. She contemplated the changes this day would bring to her life.

From this day forward, she would be known by a different name. It was an old and honored name, as was the one she was leaving behind, but it was a more powerful one. She knew from her discussions this past week with her new aunt that this was so. When one's name was Darcy, people listened. She knew this was a contributing factor to her betrothed's tendency toward arrogance and determined in her heart that she would not be that way.

After today, she would have a new residence. Actually, several. She would be Mistress of a house in London and multiple estates. There would be a large number of staff members who would answer to her. Being Mistress did not alarm her, but she knew she would miss Longbourn. It was a comfortable place for her. And she would certainly miss her family!

Her family...that was another thing that was going to change. She would exchange a large, rambunctious family for a small, quiet one. She was unsure how she would deal with that. Of course, once she bore

Decisions and Consequences

Darcy two or three children that would change. She blushed at the thought of the activities that would lead to those children. She was still unsure if she was wrong to enjoy his kisses when she was not in love with him, but she trusted her aunt's words that the marital bed would bring them closer.

Despite the size of her new family, Elizabeth was quite happy with most of its members. Lady Catherine notwithstanding, Darcy's relatives had been quite welcoming. She felt that she would be gaining another favorite aunt in Lady Matlock, who had treated her warmly from the first moment of their acquaintance. Lord Matlock, also, insisted that, since Darcy was like a son to him, so she would be a daughter.

Then there was what might possibly be the biggest change of all. After today, she would no longer be a maiden. She would be a woman

in every sense. She would share a
bed with her husband every night.
They had already discussed this,
she and Darcy. He preferred to follow the example of his parents, and
she could see no real reason to refuse him. She, who had always had
her own bedroom and slept alone,
would from this day forward sleep
with a man. She allowed herself a
few moments to fret over things like
being kicked in the night and not
having enough covers and seeing
her husband with fewer clothes.
Then she did what she had always
done when things worried her: she
allowed her courage to rise and determined that she would not be concerned about it. Married couples for
thousands of years had shared a
bed with no ill effects. There would
be a period of adjustment, she was
sure, but it would all work out in
the end. With that settled in her
mind, Elizabeth rose from her seat

and rang for a bath. She had a wedding to prepare for.

Three hours later, she was dressed and ready to go to the church. She descended the staircase to where her father waited at the bottom. Her mother and sisters had gone ahead and were already there, waiting.

"Well, Lizzy, today you leave me. I shall miss you." He took her hand and held it while he spoke. Looking down at it, he rubbed his thumb over and over the back of it as he continued. "I was, and truly remain, unhappy with the manner of your betrothal. However, I have seen that Mr. Darcy is a good man, a gentleman of high quality." He raised his eyes to his favorite daughter's tear-filled ones. "I have no fear in giving you to him. I believe you will get along well, despite your difficult beginnings. You seem to have softened toward him and he to you. He will do well by you, I am certain."

"Thank you, Papa. I believe that, as well. Now that I know Fitzwilliam better, I am more at peace with marrying him. It will be fine. Mary says we make our own happiness, and I am starting to believe she is correct." Elizabeth smiled at her father, pleased to have these last few moments alone with him.

Mr. Bennet cleared his throat. "Indeed. Well then, shall we go?" He led her out of the house and handed her into the carriage for the short ride to the church.

An hour later and the deed was done. Elizabeth Bennet signed her maiden name one last time in the church record and walked out on her new husband's arm. She felt a great sense of peace and rightness, as though she was somehow always meant to marry this man.

Darcy handed his bride into the open carriage Mrs. Bennet had insisted on, then climbed up beside her. He tossed warm blankets over their legs and wrapped his arm around her shoulder before signaling the driver to move on. The crowd that had stayed to watch their exit from the church cheered to see him embrace her.

"What are you thinking, Fitzwilliam?"

"That your mother was surely not thinking this carriage idea through when she insisted on it."

Ruefully, Elizabeth agreed. "I believe you are correct. I think she saw all the elegance and romance of it and none of the realities." She snuggled closer to him and the cold January air bit at them. "Thankfully, it is a very short trip from the church to the house!"

She was correct and within a very few minutes, they were standing in front of the fire in the dining room at Longbourn. Darcy wrapped his arms around his new wife and lowered his head. "Let me help you warm up," he whispered, and then he kissed her thoroughly, stopping only when they could hear her mother enter the house.

Mrs. Bennet, when she came into the room, was at first intent on making sure everything was set up as she had directed. Upon re assuring herself that it was as per fect as she could make it, she finally spied her daughter and son-in-law in front of the fire, standing close, his arm behind her back. She bustled over to them.

"Lizzy, what has happened to you? You are flushed. Surely you would not become ill today of all days?" Clucking her tongue, she felt Elizabeth's forehead, checking for fever when she noticed her swollen lips. "What has happened to your mouth?" Darcy cleared his throat, distracting Mrs. Bennet's attention just long enough that she could see that his were in a similar condition. Suddenly, she stopped her fussing, turning and walking away. Darcy and Elizabeth chuckled quietly.

"Well, Mr. Darcy, you certainly quieted her down."

"It was easily enough done," he replied with a grin, causing his wife to laugh out loud.

They spent an enjoyable few hours celebrating their marriage with family, friends, and neighbors. They ate as much as they could, given the fact they were interrupted almost constantly. At first, they made an effort to stand together, but before long were pulled in separate directions. Finally, Darcy, noting the time, declared it was time for them to leave. After saying goodbye to everyone, they climbed into his roomy coach and they took off.

As they began to move, Darcy once again sat beside Elizabeth and tucked blankets over their legs. This time, he added one over their torsos, as well, before wrapping his arms around her and pulling her close.

"These blankets are warm!"

"Yes, I had my coachman give them to Longbourn's cook to heat up for us. There are heated bricks in a compartment on the floor, as well. We shall have to change them when we change horses, of course, but they will help."

"Such luxury! I could get used to this," Elizabeth sighed happily.

Darcy laughed. "You will, I am sure. Come, lean against me and relax. We have a long drive ahead of us." When she did just that, laying her head on his shoulder, he bent his and captured her lips. They spent a delightful two hours kissing, only stopping for brief periods of catching their breath, until they reached the posting house. There, they went inside to warm themselves up with a pot of tea and some scones. When they were back on the road, they resumed the activity for a while, but eventually fell asleep.

Decisions and Consequences

Darcy was the first to awaken, the sudden sound of the coach's wheels on the brick pavement of London's Mayfair district bringing him out of his sleep. Upon discerning their location, he looked at his bride, her head in repose on his shoulder. *She is beautiful,* he thought. He watched her for a few more minutes, savoring the feel of her in his arms.

He had found over the course of his engagement that he rather liked holding Elizabeth. He could not explain it, but the more he touched her, the more he craved doing so. Being a man of introspection, he analyzed it. Yet, he could not identify the root cause of this deep need. It almost defied explanation. In the end, he gave up on it and accepted it as fact. He thought at the time, *I am marrying the girl, and then it will be completely acceptable to hold her as often as I wish.*

Before too long, though, he ceased his observation of her and woke her up. She had just enough time to straighten her hair and make herself as presentable as possible before they stopped in front of Darcy House. She looked out the window at the elegant, four story townhome.

"It's beautiful, Fitzwilliam. So elegant!"

Darcy smiled. "I am glad you approve."

The footman opened the door to allow Darcy to exit. He stepped out, looking quickly over the house before turning to hand Elizabeth out. He escorted her up the steps and into the home, where a complement of staff was lined up to greet them.

Elizabeth was a little nervous about this part of the day. However, that courage that always rose within her came to the fore again and if one were to ask the Darcy House staff later if she seemed intimidated, they would deny it. She greeted them with a friendly smile as her new husband began to introduce her.

"Mrs. Darcy, I am pleased to introduce you to Darcy House's butler, Mr. Baxter, and its housekeeper, Mrs. Bishop."

"I am so pleased to meet you. Mr. Darcy has told me how much he relies on the two of you to run his home smoothly. I know I can depend upon you, as well, as I learn the duties of Mistress of the house."

The two faithful servants were relieved at the new Mrs. Darcy's obvious sincerity and warmth of manner. They had feared the woman Mr. Darcy would marry, especially after he had hosted the Bingleys for dinner a few times. That he would offer for Miss Bingley was their worst fear. She was ungenerous with the staff, to the point of meanness. The maids were afraid of her, each and every one, and the cook had threatened to quit when she tried to interfere with the kitchen operations. Had Mr. Darcy married Miss Bingley, his butler and house-keeper would have had to replace the entire staff, they were certain.

After introducing her to the remaining servants, including her new maid, Jenny, Darcy and Eliza-beth retired to their rooms to re-fresh themselves. Darcy left in-structions for a meal to be served to them in their sitting room.

Chapter 11

An hour later, Darcy knocked on Elizabeth's dressing room door. When she bid him enter, he opened it and stuck his head in.

"Our meal is ready, Elizabeth."

"Thank you, Fitzwilliam. You are welcome to come in. I am dressed." She smiled at him in the mirror of her dressing table.

He entered the room, shutting the door behind him. His wife sat at the small table, dressed in a simple but elegant emerald green gown. Her maid was putting the finishing touches on her coiffure, a chignon that looked like it was barely held up. He knew from previous experience with Elizabeth's hair that there would be numerous pins holding it in place. His fingers fairly itched to remove them, but he bid himself to wait at least until they had eaten.

"You look fetching in that gown, Mrs. Darcy."

Elizabeth gave him a wry look, as though she suspected he might like her better without it, and simply thanked him for the compliment Rising, she took his outstretched hand and allowed him to escort her to their shared sitting room.

For Darcy, the evening was passing interminably slowly. After keeping his urges under good regulation for so many years, having license to act on them made him eager to do so. The kissing they had indulged in on the way to town had only inflamed those urges. He had to remind himself that Elizabeth was gently-born and quite possibly nervous about the prospect of being intimate with him. He obviously did not know the female perspective on this kind of thing, but she was a lady. He must treat her as such, at least for now.

Seating her at the small table, Darcy began to serve her from the dishes placed on the table. They ate heartily, as they had had very little all day and were hungry. Finally, they finished and covered the rem nants. Elizabeth sat on the settee in front of the fireplace while Darcy rang for a servant to remove the trays, then sat beside her. They remained on opposite ends, talking quietly, until the servants had cleared the table and were dismissed for the night. At that point, he moved to sit closer and they began kissing as they had in the carriage. This time, however, their hands started to roam. A short time later, Darcy rose, lifting his bride in his arms, and carried her to his bed.

It was very late the next day before the servants were called for again. As her maid attended her, helping her wash and dress in a

271

simple morning gown, Elizabeth thought about the previous night. To say she enjoyed herself was an understatement.

Darcy had been wonderful. He was careful and considerate, though obviously eager. There had been a few fumbling moments along the way for both of them, but the sense of fulfillment, the explosive crest they both had fallen over, was worth every moment of discomfort. Waking early this morning, entwined with him and watching him sleep, she was struck by a sense of belonging, as though their souls were now intertwined. *Maybe this is what Aunt Maddie meant,* she thought, *about our souls being tied together.*

They broke their fast in the sitting room, declining to leave their suite. They fell into bed once again after eating, this time not bothering to call for a servant. Darcy's valet, Smith, had quietly cleaned the mess up and took it upon himself to inform Mrs. Bishop that all meals should be served in the Master's Suite until further notice.

For three days, Darcy and Elizabeth slept, ate, and made love in their rooms. On the fourth day, they finally emerged long enough for a tour of the house. The maids quickly caught on to leave any room in which the couple entered, for there was much kissing and laughter involved in this tour, and suspicions of more, though no one said that out loud. Every staff member was delighted to hear the master's laugh booming through the house. That the new mistress was the cause only endeared her to them.

When the Darcys emerged from their rooms on the fourteenth day of their marriage, it was with the knowledge that their honeymoon was over. The knocker would go up on the door and they would attend a dinner this evening hosted by Lord and Lady Matlock.

Decisions and Consequences

"You do realize that not only did we miss Twelfth Night, we did not get to church on Epiphany?" Elizabeth was spreading jam over her toast as she spoke. They had decided to break their fast in their sitting room every day, unless they had guests. It was the only way they knew to preserve a bit of the honeymoon feeling.

"Yes, we did at that. I am sure the Lord knows that we were obeying his command to cleave to each other."

Elizabeth laughed. "Fitzwilliam!"

He looked up from his plate, innocence shining from every pore. "What?"

Rolling her eyes, his wife responded, "Do not be blasphemous."

"How is it blasphemous? Do you think He does not know what we have been doing in here for the last fortnight?"

"I am quite certain He does."

"And are we not to cleave to each other now that we are married?"

"Well, I am unclear as to the precise wording, but yes, I do believe that is the gist of the verse."

"My point is made. We were obeying God's command and are therefore exempt from any consequence that may arise from missing church on Epiphany."

Elizabeth laughed. "Very well, Husband. Should the rector visit, I shall be sure he understands that."

"Well, now, I would not go that far. Though, I am quite certain that should the bishop, or even my godfather the archbishop, notice that we missed service, they will also assume the same."

"Silly man."

They separated for the first time that morning, Darcy to deal with business in his study and Elizabeth to begin learning the household accounts and routines. They kept busy enough to not notice the movement of the hands on the clock, and soon it was time for tea and to prepare for their outing.

Darcy once again knocked on his wife's dressing room door. This time, when she bid him enter, he did so right away. She was ready to leave, dressed to perfection in a shiny gown in dark purple silk with silver satin trim. Her hair was intricately arranged in braids woven with ribbons to match the trim on the dress. The square neckline was modest, showing just a hint of cleavage. Darcy, staring at that tiny bit of exposed skin and knowing what was underneath the gown, felt a sudden surge of jealousy that anyone should see any part of her. He tamped it down, however, knowing as he did that she would be going home with him and that no one else would ever see her unclothed.

Elizabeth gazed up at her husband, seeing the darkness in his eyes that she knew meant he wanted her, but also seeing something else that she could not recognize. It was not until he seized her around the middle, pulling her to him and growling, "Mine.'" in her ear that she began to comprehend he might be feeling some jealousy that other men might see her bosom. When he claimed her mouth in a searing kiss, she knew. She kissed him back, attempting to reassure him that she was indeed his, just as he was hers. After several moments, they breathlessly pulled away from each other, Darcy resting his forehead on hers.

Breathing heavily, Darcy admitted, "I do not want to share you. I am bothered by your décolletage and tormented by the knowledge that other men will see it."

"Fitzwilliam," Elizabeth whispered. "I never wish to share what we have done with anyone else. You need not fear someone turning my head. I am quite satisfied with the husband I have."

Darcy stilled as that word bounded around in his mind. Satisfied. He satisfied her. *Wait, Darcy,* his mind warned. *Be assured of her meaning before you gloat.* "I satisfied you?"

"In every way."

Feeling his chest swell with manly pride, Darcy grinned. *I satisfied her.* Lifting his head from hers, he straightened, squaring his shoulders. Let other men look, for that is all they could do. *He* satisfied her. "Come, Wife, let us show these gentlemen what they will forever be doomed to miss."

Elizabeth laughed as she tucked her hand in his elbow and let him lead her down the stairs.

~~~***~~~

At Matlock House, just two streets over from Darcy House, Lord and Lady Matlock waited, eager to introduce their new niece to their friends. They had not heard from

Darcy since the wedding, but had driven past his house earlier today to see the door knocker up, so they knew for certain he and Elizabeth were attending. They stood in readiness to greet them as soon as they heard the knock on their door.

"Mr. and Mrs. Fitzwilliam Darcy," their butler, Mr. Anderson, announced as the guests of honor arrived.

Lady Matlock, normally poised and composed in all situations, held her hands out to Elizabeth with a large smile wreathing her face. "Dear Elizabeth! You look stunning." She leaned in to receive a kiss to her cheek and give one in return. "Is my nephew treating you well? You look very happy."

"Yes, he is, Aunt Audra. Very well indeed."

The two women smiled at each other and then turned to their husbands.

Decisions and Consequences

"Aunt Audra." Darcy bowed to her and his uncle. "Do I detect some excitement in your normally unflappable demeanor?"

She slapped his arm with the fan in her hand. "Do stop teasing me. Of course, I am excited. 'Tis not every day my favorite nephew and his beautiful new bride grace my home with their presence. I am eager to show the two of you off."

"Yes," Lord Matlock interjected, "she has been driving the entire household to Bedlam today. She wants this evening to be perfect." He bowed over Elizabeth's hand. "I am delighted to see you, dear girl. You are a breath of fresh air."

"Thank you, Uncle Henry. I am happy to be here."

Looking at the ornate clock on the mantle, Lady Matlock began urging them all to the entrance hall to form a receiving line. Georgiana came down, greeting her brother and sister enthusiastically before taking

280

her place. She would be allowed to join the party, mainly because it was in honor of Darcy's marriage but also because she would be coming out in another year or so and small events such as this were perfectly acceptable for her to attend.

They were no more than ready when the first of the guests arrived. Elizabeth was introduced to all of the Matlocks' relatives, friends, neighbors, political allies, and not a few political enemies. Also invited were Darcy's godfather and his Darcy cousins.

The last to arrive were the Gardiners, who had become fast friends with Lord and Lady Matlock while still in Hertfordshire. It turned out that Lady Matlock and Mrs. Gardiner assisted the same charities, and so had much in common. Both being ladies in possession of large quantities of common sense, little tolerance for fools, and enough discernment to easily identify said fools, they quickly took measure of each other and found a kindred spirit. Their husbands were much the same, quickly finding things in common and spending time together. It was a natural thing to invite them, regardless of their social status, given those friendships and the fact that they shared a niece and nephew.

The guests all mingled for a while before being called in to dine. As usual in such situations, the Darcys needed to separate. With Lady Matlock on one side of her and Mrs. Gardiner on the other, Elizabeth made her way around the room, speaking to everyone and thanking them for sharing this special event with her and her husband. Most of the guests were predisposed to like her, as the Matlocks had spent the previous fortnight talking her up to everyone they knew. There were a few who were the opposite—determined not to like her because she had captured the prize they wanted: Darcy. Having already known this was a likely possibility, Elizabeth was ready. She was charming to everyone. Those who attended with a desire to like her were thrilled with her. Those who came with the firm belief they could never like her rebuffed her efforts, but could not shake her no matter how they tried. And, most gratifying of all to Elizabeth, were those who arrived at Matlock House determined not to like her but who found they could not avoid it, and by the end of the evening, they were reaching out to her in friendship.

When the Darcys were preparing to leave, Lady Matlock hugged both of them, telling them over and over how well she believed the night went and how proud she was of both of them. After gaining Elizabeth's consent for a shopping trip two days hence, she let them go.

Decisions and Consequences

They finally arrived home in the wee hours of the morning, exhausted. They fell into bed, and after a quick loving went to sleep, not waking until late the next day.

~~~***~~~

That evening, Georgiana joined them for dinner. Having her in the house reminded Elizabeth of the promise she had made to her sister Mary.

"Fitzwilliam?" she asked.

"Yes, Elizabeth?"

"Do you recall we told Mary she could come stay with us for the season?"

"I do. Are you thinking of having her this season?"

"I am. Do you object?"

"Not at all."

"Oh," Georgiana interjected, "I enjoyed meeting Miss Mary at the wedding, and I am certain we would get along very well. We have music in common, after all."

"You do not mind sharing me?" Elizabeth smiled at her.

"Well, I do, but since she was your sister before and you are the mistress now with many responsibilities, I cannot imagine I would have to share you often. In fact, my guess is that I will have two sisters here, because I know that Miss Mary and I, with our shared loved of you, will become very close." She smiled triumphantly, causing Elizabeth to laugh.

"Excellent!" She turned to Darcy. "So, have I your permission to invite her?"

Darcy smiled at his wife, knowing he could deny her nothing. "Very well. Invite Miss Mary." He stood to leave, and as he pulled out her chair so she could rise, he leaned down for a lingering kiss. "Shall we retire to another room?"

She caressed his cheek. "Yes, perhaps Georgiana can play for us before she returns to Matlock House."

Decisions and Consequences

The three of them retired to the music room, where Georgiana played for them. Elizabeth wrote letters, one to Jane, one to Mary to invite her to visit, and one to her father, assuring him of his good health and asking he send Mary to her whenever it was convenient.

~~~***~~~

Unknown to the Darcys, someone was watching their home. He knew the date of their marriage and that they had honeymooned in London. He followed them to Matlock House and was watching from the park when they arrived home.

A ragged, hungry, and dirty George Wickham had spent weeks fighting for survival after deserting the militia. For a time, he had remained just one step ahead of the officers sent to hunt him down and return him to Colonel Forster. Those officers seemed to have given

286

up the chase, but he knew to be cautious nonetheless. He longed for a hot bath and clean clothes.

The weeks spent on the run had hardened the anger Wickham had felt at Darcy's interference in Meryton. Not normally given to plotting revenge, he felt as though Darcy had taken away his last good chance at having the life he deserved, and he wanted the man to pay. Not left out of this new hatred was Miss Elizabeth Bennet, now Elizabeth Darcy. It was her disbelief of his tale of woe and her determination to go to her betrothed with it that led to his downfall. While he watched their home, Wickham thought and planned.

He considered and threw away several ideas. The first thing he thought of was to try to get Georgiana again. She had believed him once, and she was young and foolish, or she had been. However, the more he thought, the less likely it seemed that she would fall into his trap twice. Besides, she was at Matlock House and closely watched. All the servants there knew who he was and what he looked like, and he was aware of their orders to detain him and call the Magistrates should he show his face there.

His next thought was to get to the Darcys by ruining one of Elizabeth's sisters. Lydia would do quite nicely for it. She, like Georgiana, was young and foolish, and her head was even more easily turned than Georgiana's was. Unfortunately, that scheme would involve returning to Meryton where, again, everyone knew who he was. He was certain he would not make it to Longbourn before he was seen and arrested.

That left harming the Darcys themselves. There were a number of possibilities there, and any number of locations. He could do something here in London, or he could wait until they went to Pemberley. He supposed, though, that he should decide what the appropriate penance should be and go from there.

In the end, Wickham decided on what seemed like the easiest scheme to get away with. He was in possession of a pair of pistols, items that he had yet to pawn. He decided he would kidnap Elizabeth, knowing Darcy would pay him to get her back. After all, he had paid every other time Wickham had done something. This time, however, Darcy would get back a dead wife. This would make his revenge complete. Now settled on a plan, Wickham returned day after day to watch Darcy House, waiting for his opportunity.

Finally, the day came just a week later. He watched the carriage being brought around. Moving close enough that he could hear what the coachman and groom said, he was elated to see Elizabeth come out of the house alone and enter it. He began to follow it as it moved slowly through the streets. Knowing it was headed to Bond Street, he knew he must move quickly.

The carriage came to a stop at an intersection just a block away from its destination, so that a dray carrying milk could pass. Wickham took his opportunity then, opening up the carriage door and jumping in. To his shock, Elizabeth was not alone.

Darcy was sitting beside her, having surprised her with his presence when she thought he was tied up with business. They had spent little time together since the Matlock's dinner. Though they made love every night and slept entwined, they both missed the long conversations and afternoons spent reading or playing chess that had characterized their honeymoon period. So on this day, he had snuck out of the house through the kitchen and installed himself in the carriage, much to the amusement of his staff. His

290

wife's soft cry of delight at finding him there made all the subterfuge worth it.

When Wickham leaped into the carriage wielding his pistol, all three of them froze. It was Darcy who recovered his wits first, throwing himself across the seat both to protect Elizabeth and to disarm the man who was fast becoming his mortal enemy. No words were spoken as the men wrestled with the firearm. Darcy was, at first, triumphant to realize he had gained the upper hand, but then saw Wickham pull a second gun out of his pocket and cock the hammer. Darcy yelled and cocked the gun in his own hand just as Wickham fired. He jerked back a bit from the impact of the bullet, firing as he did so. He heard Elizabeth cry out, but smoke filled the carriage.

The door to the equipage opened, allowing the smoke to begin clearing. Darcy could not check on

Decisions and Consequences

his wife without being sure of Wickham's location and condition, so he kept his eyes trained in that direction even as he called Elizabeth's name.

Finally able to see that Wickham was not moving, Darcy told his coachman to call the Magistrates, knowing there would be an investigation. He turned to see why his wife had not answered him only to find her unconscious and bleeding on the seat behind him.

"Elizabeth!" He leaned his face close to hers and was relieved to feel her breath on his face. "McAlister," he called to his coachman, "come quickly!" When the man appeared, he began barking orders. "Send a footman to retrieve the physician. Mrs. Darcy is hurt. Then, send another to Darcy House to alert Mrs. Bishop and to Matlock House to tell my aunt. Oh, and someone needs to go to Gracechurch Street and let the Gardiners know."

"Yes, sir," McAlister replied, turning to shout orders to the servants.

In the carriage, Darcy glanced again at Wickham. Seeing the man remained unmoving and with a large, bloody hole in his chest, he returned his attention to Elizabeth. Examining her more carefully, he tried not to panic at the amount of blood he saw. It appeared the bullet had entered her upper chest, near her collarbone. The more he saw, the more worried he became. She was not a large woman, his Elizabeth. Surely she could not afford to lose much blood. He felt her shoulder, relieved that nothing seemed to be broken. Quickly, he removed his cravat and pressed it against her wound. When the flow of blood slowed, he knelt on the floor of the carriage in front of her, maintaining the pressure on her shoulder the best he could. He was not feeling

Decisions and Consequences

well himself, but he would see his wife taken care of first.

"McAlister?"

"Yes, Mr. Darcy?"

"You sent someone for the doctor?"

"Yes, sir."

"What is taking him so blasted long then?"

"I know not, sir, but I promised the boy an extra crown were he to return quickly and have the doctor with him."

"Very good."

After a pause of several minutes, McAlister, who could see the blood and the tear in his master's greatcoat, spoke again. "Mr. Darcy?"

"Yes, McAlister," Darcy responded wearily.

"Perhaps, sir, you might rest a while and let me take care of the mistress? You are hurt, as well. You cannot be any good to Mrs. Darcy if you are unconscious yourself." He swallowed as he finished. It was not in his nature to speak so to his employer, but over the course of his many years with the Darcys, he had come to look upon them as he might his own family. It would be devastating to more than just him if either the master or the mistress passed on as a result of today's disaster.

"I will not. Thank you, McAlister, for offering. You are a good man and a fine employee, but she is my wife and I shall see to her. Do not be concerned for me. I am tougher than I appear." He grinned just a little at his own joke, and McAlister chuckled.

"Aye, sir. I see that. Very well, sir."

Chapter 12

Not a quarter hour later, the physician and Magistrate appeared simultaneously. The doctor ascertained that Elizabeth was alive, and seeing that Darcy had applied pressure to the wound to slow the bleeding, insisted on looking at Darcy's wound before he allowed either of them to be moved. A few minutes later, another of the Darcy coaches arrived to transport the couple to their home. Darcy was impatient, causing him to be cold and curt with the doctor. However, the man would not be moved from his course and so Darcy gave in, though he would not be pleased until his Elizabeth was in their bed and her wound being attended to.

Finally, in his home and after assuring himself that his wife had received the best care possible, he allowed his own injuries to be seen to. That done, he climbed into bed with his wife, pulling her into his arms. He was concerned that she had not regained full consciousness yet, and though she had wavered in and out on the trip home, he hoped her current state was just a result of the laudanum the doctor administered so he could remove the bullet. As he held her close, he whispered endearments to her, begging her to return to him. "Elizabeth, Sweetheart, wake up. My beautiful wife, come back to me." He kissed her forehead.

Suddenly, Darcy came to a startling though not unwelcome realization. He had fallen in love with his wife. He held her tighter as thoughts of what could have happened today filled his mind.

"Oh, Elizabeth, I could have lost you," he whispered. He kissed her head. "Please wake up and let me know you will be well."

Darcy remained awake as long as he could manage, continually caressing her face and shoulder and kissing her. "I love you, I love you," he softly repeated, tears running down his face in a sudden flood. Eventually, his own injury and the exhaustion from the event caused him to fall asleep. He woke hours later to the sound of his wife's moans. Instantly, he was alert.

"Elizabeth?"

So softly he had to strain to hear it, she replied. "Fitzwilliam."

"Oh, thank the Lord you are awake! I have been so worried about you!" He gathered her close once more. "I need to tell you that I love you, Elizabeth. When I consider how things could have ended..." He shuddered and then gently kissed her lips, her cheek, and her brow. "I do not want to think about having to continue living my life alone." After a moment longer of just holding her and being glad she was alive and awake, Darcy pulled back enough to examine her more closely. "Is there anything I can get you, my love?"

"Water."

"Of course." He made to rise, the sharp pain in his arm recalling to him his own injury. "Give me just a second, my love."

Carefully, he let go of his wife and lifted himself to a sitting position. He breathed in deeply and held it, letting it out slowly as the pain receded. He had not allowed the physician to give him laudanum when the gunshot wound in his arm was stitched up. It was a flesh wound; the bullet had grazed the skin. Darcy refused to be medicated to the point that he could not care for his Elizabeth. Reaching for the bedside stand, he poured a tumbler of water from the pitcher left there and turned back to her. Realizing that she was prone and could not drink that way, he set it back on the stand and carefully lifted her up, leaning her against his chest. Gritting his teeth against the pain, he reached around and grasped the tumbler once again, this time successfully holding it to Elizabeth's lips and allowing her to drink.

When she was finished, and he had put the glass back on the stand, she looked earnestly into his eyes.

"You are injured."

Darcy nodded. "The bullet but grazed me. It is nothing."

Elizabeth tried to lift her hand to his face, grimacing at the realization that her arm was immobile. "I am injured, as well?"

"Yes, my love. I am so sorry I was unable to protect you." Darcy buried his face in her hair, ashamed that he had not been able to prevent her injury.

"Shhh. Tell me what happened?"

"Wickham jumped into our carriage."

"Wickham!" Her eyes wandered over his shoulder as she searched her memories for what might have happened. "I remember noise and smoke." She looked into his eyes once more. "You got the gun."

Darcy swallowed. "Yes, but he had a second one. He fired before I could, and the doctor believes the bullet hit me before it reached you. Your injury could have been so much worse." He closed his eyes. The pain the mere thought of that caused was intense.

"Fitzwilliam." When he looked at her, she continued, "I am well. I will be well. I am not going anywhere. I love you." She smiled at his look of joy.

"Oh, my love." He tenderly pressed his lips to hers once more. "Let us settle down into the bed and rest. I would not have you become over-tired."

The pair of them went back to sleep, and were cuddled together when their families came to check on them.

~~~***~~~

While Darcy and Elizabeth were still in the carriage waiting for the physician, Lady Matlock was sitting in her private sitting room. Anderson knocked on the door, and upon gaining entrance, informed her that a Darcy footman was belowstairs, reporting that Elizabeth was injured.

"Injured? How?" Lady Matlock rose in alarm from her place on the settee, one hand pressed to her chest, the other to her mouth.

"He says she was shot, as was Mr. Darcy. He asks that you travel immediately to Darcy House."

"Yes, I shall! Call for the carriage, please, Anderson."

"Immediately, madam. If you would like to speak to the footman, I sent him to the kitchen. He was gasping for breath. I believe he ran the entire route."

"I would very much like to speak to him. Thank you."

She rushed out the door and down the back stairs to the kitchen When she arrived at her destination, she so badly shocked a maid, who had never heard of the mistress using the back stairs or even that she knew where they were, that she dropped a basket of vegetables meant for the evening meal. The startled staff, including the still red-faced footman, rose at her entrance.

Stopping dead in her tracks, as though suddenly realizing that her behavior was less than ladylike, she focused her gaze on the messenger.

"What has happened?"

He bowed then responded. "The master surprised the mistress and hid in the carriage; he wanted to go to the bookstore with her. Said he had not spent nearly enough time with her. When we were just a couple streets from our destination, we had to stop at an intersection for a wagon to pass on the cross street. It was then it happened. Somcone ran up, opened the door, and jumped in. We heard Mr. Darcy fighting the man, but by the time we got to the door, we heard gunshots. There's a man, the one that jumped in, who is dead, and both the master and mistress are shot, as well. I think the mistress must be in worse shape, for the master was still speaking and Mrs. Darcy was silent."

Lady Matlock nodded sharply. "Thank you." Turning to the housekeeper and cook, who hovered nearby, she said, "Send someone to the House of Lords. We need Lord Matlock at Darcy House. I am leaving directly; I shall meet him there. Cook, if things are as bad as I fear they must be, we will eat at Darcy House."

"Madam," Anderson called from the doorway to the mews. "I

have had the carriage brought to the back door. It is ready."

"Very good." She swept through the kitchen, accepting her pelisse, bonnet, and gloves from the butler and hurrying outside to board her carriage. She was the first to arrive at Darcy House, followed within thirty minutes by first her husband and then the Darcys themselves. Seeing her nephew carrying a very still and pale Elizabeth caused her fear to rise to new levels.

The very efficient Darcy staff had already begun preparations to receive their injured employers. Lady Matlock had reviewed them, approving most and adding a few others she thought might be necessary. "It is better to be safe than sorry," she explained to Mrs. Bishop. When Darcy came striding in with his burden, warm water was already being carried upstairs and the bed turned down to receive them.

The Master of Pemberley never broke his stride, despite his aunt and uncle standing in his entrance hall, calling out to him. They were forced to hurry after him and the physician who had entered with him. They caught up just as he entered the master's chambers. Lord Matlock was the last to cross the threshold. He quietly closed the door and moved to stand behind his wife, who was at the end of the bed observing as the doctor prepared for his examination, and Darcy and Jenny tore at Elizabeth's gown to expose her wound.

Lady Matlock gasped when she saw the bleeding mess that was her newest niece's shoulder. Her husband's arm came up around her shoulders, pulling her into him as she buried her face in his neck, and bringing his free arm around to completely encase her in his embrace. Stoically the earl watched as the doctor cleaned the area, then administered laudanum to Elizabeth. He had seen worse injuries in his time in the army, before he ascended to the earldom, but knew that his injuries was very bad. It was difficult to watch as this young woman he thought of as a daughter was examined.

Mrs. Bishop soon bustled in with warm water, followed by a maid carrying towels. The doctor began to insist that the earl and countess leave, and take Darcy with them. All of them refused, Darcy most adamantly.

"Absolutely not," he stated in his most severe Master of Pemberley voice. "I will not leave her side until I am certain everything has been done for her that can be." Between his cold voice and even colder glare, the doctor soon backed down and allowed him to stay. As for the Matlocks, they were peers. He shrugged, knowing they could and would do as they wished. As long as they stayed out of his way and did not faint, he could ignore them.

Soon the point became unimportant, as a soft knock came to the door, and Darcy's butler, Mr. Baxter, entered the room to speak softly to Lord Matlock. Nodding to the senior servant, he whispered to his wife. She glanced at Darcy, then held tightly to her husband's hand as he led her from the room.

Once in the hall, he informed her as they strode down the stairs that Mrs. Gardiner was in the drawing room. When the door opened, the women cried out to each other and rushed to embrace.

"How is she?"

"The physician is with her. He is digging a bullet out of her shoulder and then will close the wound. When he is done, he will give us a report," she looked to her husband. "Will he not, Henry?"

"Yes, my love, I should imagine so."

"And Fitzwilliam?"

"He has an injury to his upper arm but refuses treatment until Elizabeth has been taken care of. From what we have been able to see, it is not as deep as hers," Lord Matlock informed her. He had been the only one to look closely at Darcy's wound. Audra's face had been buried in his neck and Darcy had been standing with his uninjured arm toward them when it was not; she would not have anything of value to add.

Mrs. Gardiner nodded numbly. It was such a shock to hear of something so horrible happening to any of her dear family, especially those just starting out in life.

"Mrs. Gardiner?" Lord Matlock's voice softly asking her name drew her focus. "Has Gardiner been informed?"

She nodded. "Yes, I sent one of our footmen to the warehouse to alert him. I am unsure, however, of when he can get away. I asked him to come as soon as he could."

"Very good."

Lady Matlock and her friend were seated together on a sofa, their hands clinging together, comforting each other. A quiet knock was heard and Lord Matlock bid entrance.

Mrs. Bishop entered with a heavily laden tea tray. "I thought those who were waiting might require sustenance. I assume more than just you will be arriving soon, my lady." Mrs. Bishop was a motherly woman who had raised three children of her own while maintaining employment as a maid. She had risen to the position of housekeeper here years ago, not long after her husband had died and before Old Mr. Darcy had passed. She had seen the Darcy children grow from small children to the people they were now, and that instinct and desire to mother them was strong. To Mrs. Bishop, and thankfully to the cook, who otherwise would have felt herself grievously used, food was the best way to comfort a body in this situation.

"Thank you, Mrs. Bishop. We will indeed need something to keep our strength up while we wait." Smiling at the housekeeper, Lady Matlock began to pour out tea for the three of them. She was still pouring when her second son arrived. Entering the room along with him was Mr. Gardiner and Mary Bennet, who had reached the house at the exact same moment.

"Edward!" Mrs. Gardiner rose from her seat and rushed to her husband.

Wrapping her tightly in his embrace, Gardiner looked over her head at the other couple. Without being asked, Lord Matlock explained what they knew as Lady Matlock went to Mary to lead to her a sofa and hold her while she quietly cried. Gardiner nodded. After a few moments, the couple separated and sat to wait with their friends and niece. The room was mostly quiet; just a murmur here and there and the clink of china cups being set down marred the stillness.

Finally, after what felt to the group like hours, the physician came down to talk to them.

"Both have had their wounds stitched. I have given instructions for their care to their servants. Mr. Darcy's wound was a flesh wound. I believe the bullet grazed his arm before it hit Mrs. Darcy. Probably saved her life, that. As it is, I had to dig around a bit to find the pieces of the bullet, but I believe I got them all. Both of them need to be watched closely for any sign of fever or infection. I will call around tomorrow morning to check on them."

"Thank you, sir," Lord Matlock began. "Do you know anything about the shooter?"

"Dead. Hole in his chest. I suspect it was instant."

Matlock nodded. "Thank you, sir."

Once the doctor had gone, the group collectively released a breath that none realized they had been holding. Looking at each other, they silently wondered what to do next. Finally, Mrs. Gardiner spoke up.

"I should like to see Lizzy, if I may."

"An excellent idea, Maddie," Lady Matlock exclaimed. She stood, then hesitated, gesturing her husband and Mr. Gardiner out of the room. "Their sleeping arrangements..."

Mrs. Gardiner nodded, understanding what her friend was trying to say. She turned to Mary. "My dear, I do not know what you have been taught about how married couples sleep..."

Surprised, Mary's eyebrows rose. "Their sleeping arrangements?

Why, do not married couples sleep together in the same room?"

Now it was Lady Matlock's turn to be astonished. "Not necessarily. How do you know this, Miss Mary?"

Mary blushed and explained. "I have never been one to sleep for long periods, and the walls at Longbourn are not as thick as one might think. My room is next door to my mother's, and I often hear my parents talking and making noise after we have all gone to bed, and again in the mornings as they rise for the day. I assumed that all couples shared a room. It seems I was wrong?"

Mrs. Gardiner was the one to respond. "No, my dear, there are many married couples who share a room and a bed every night. There are others who do not, as Lady Matlock indicated. I do not know for certain that your sister and brother do, but they have not been married

Decisions and Consequences

long, and I believe it is safe to say they do, at this point. We simply do not want you to be shocked by what you may see."

"Oh. Thank you, Aunt. My desire to see Lizzy far outweighs any concern I have for her private business and how she conducts her marriage. I will not be shocked, I promise."

"Very well, then, let us go up."

The gentlemen were waiting in the hall, and the five of them silently ascended the staircase. Upon reaching the Master's Suite, they nodded to the footman posted beside the door before entering. They dismissed Jenny and Smith for the time being, instructing them to return in an hour. Then, they sat, observing Darcy and Elizabeth as they slept.

The injured Darcys slept fitfully that night. The next day, both had slight fevers; Darcy's fell quickly but Elizabeth's began to rise. His panic roused the entire household. When the doctor arrived to check on them, he ordered laudanum in Darcy's tea to calm him. He would have liked to have the couple in separate beds, but when Darcy fought him on it and was supported by the combined Matlock and Gardiner families, he backed down and allowed the man to care for his wife as he saw fit.

For three days, Elizabeth's fever raged. Not only were their personal servants involved in nursing her, but both families were, as well. Darcy was kept medicated most of the time, but remained in the bed with his wife, holding her close. He finally awoke, his brain fuzzy and his mouth dry, shortly before her fever broke. By the time he was aware enough to remember how ill she was, her skin was cooler, though she had sweat through her nightshift and sheets. Weak as he was after three days with no food, Darcy was forced to allow others to

Decisions and Consequences

bathe and redress Elizabeth while he went to his dressing room and allowed his valet to help him clean up, as well. His relief, when he got back in the bed and saw she was awake, was great. They were brought some broth and tea, which he helped his wife eat, and they settled back down to sleep. This time, more naturally.

They slept for the better part of two more days, their bodies requiring the rest so they could heal. During that time, they received several visits from his aunt and uncle as well as hers. Mary was tireless in her efforts to assist, and his sister also came to sit with them. Georgiana had not been told at first of her sister and brother's injuries. Lord and Lady Matlock were concerned she might not be of an age to deal well with such trauma. However, their son Richard, who was one of Georgiana's guardians, was adamant not only that she be told, but

318

that she be allowed to assist in tending them if she wished.

"She must grow up at some point, Mother. Imagine how she would feel, orphaned already, to discover that her only remaining family was dead of a fever. Even if Darcy were to survive, Georgiana would be devastated to lose the sister she always wanted. All she has spoken about for the last two or three months is Elizabeth. And, she has an excellent example in Miss Mary. That young lady is rarely away from the sickroom. Her caring nature is highlighted in a way it might not be otherwise. Only good can come of my ward being witness to that kind of devotion."

Eventually, his parents gave in, and he himself delivered the news to his young cousin. Though she was obviously frightened, Georgiana put on a brave face, insisting she see her brother and sister. Darcy left the bed long enough to greet his sister and refresh himself while she sat with Elizabeth for a while. After that, Georgiana sat in a chair just inside their sitting room doorway and out of sight of the bed, and read to them for a long time from one of the books on the shelf by the fireplace. Although she had been scheduled to stay at Matlock House another fortnight, Georgiana moved back to Darcy House the next day, to be closer to Darcy and Elizabeth and to help entertain them while they recovered.

The Gardiners were also daily visitors, and once the Darcys were out of bed, they brought their children to visit their favorite cousin and her husband.

Darcy continued to hover over Elizabeth to ensure her continued good health. There was nothing she did not need that he did not anticipate, or, at least, it seemed that way to her. As independent as she was known to be, she normally would not have tolerated it half so well, but with the acknowledgment of their mutual love and the worry Darcy seemed unable to hide, she gracefully accepted every gesture.

Chapter 13

One afternoon, about a month following the attack on their persons, Elizabeth received a letter from Jane. She eagerly opened it, as she was anxious to learn of her family.

"Oh," she said to Darcy, who was stretched out in the bed beside her, "it sounds so lovely!"

"What does, Sweetheart?"

"They are at the Lakes. She describes the cliffs and hills to me. They must be very beautiful!"

"Indeed, they are. I shall take you to see them when you are better."

Elizabeth smiled. He was such a dear man. "Truly, Fitzwilliam?"

"Truly. Anything the keeper of my heart desires is hers. All she need do is ask."

Laughing, Elizabeth leaned over and caressed his lips with her own. "Silly man."

Smiling at her with that tender look she was coming to cherish, he asked, "Do you regret missing the wedding?"

She sighed. "In some ways, yes. But, we were not well enough to travel, and Jane understands that. She says that she and Bingley will come to see us after Easter. Bingley wishes to enjoy part of the season in town."

"I rather suspect he wishes to marry his sister off more than anything."

Nodding, Elizabeth admitted it was likely so. "I hope she does indeed find someone. I am certain it will be a challenge for Bingley, and yet, there are men out there looking for wives who, I am certain, would welcome the challenge Miss Bingley presents?"

Darcy snorted. "I am sure there are. I was not one of them."

"And glad I am for it!" She smiled slyly at him. "Do you not find *me* a challenge, my love?"

Darcy rolled his eyes. "I know how I must answer this one." Looking deep into her eyes he added, "Indeed, precious wife of mine, you do present a challenge. I am challenged to maintain my countenance on a daily basis while you do things like," he leaned over and kissed her. "Lean." Kiss. "Over." Kiss. "A." Kiss. "Table." Kiss. Another kiss, long and slow. Releasing her lips, he added, "And teasing me with those tempting lips. And running your hand over my posterior. And giving me that certain look when we are not alone." He kissed her one more time, deeply. "Oh, yes, I find you quite the challenge." Jane's letter was forgotten for an hour or so.

~~~***~~~

Decisions and Consequences

That night, as they cuddled in bed, Elizabeth began to ask Darcy about Georgiana.

"She will turn seventeen this year, will she not?"

"She will. I had planned on having her come out next season, in January."

"Probably wise. She is yet a bit immature. I think it would be best to give her those extra months to grow. You made an excellent choice for a companion. Mrs. Annesley is a good model for her to follow, and such a wonderful teacher!"

"She is. The colonel and I are quite satisfied with her. We had thought, upon my engagement, to dismiss her, since we now have you in the family. Given the events since our marriage, I am glad we did not. I would not want to burden you with taking care of my sister when you should be recovering."

"Well, she is now my sister, too, but I do appreciate your

thoughtfulness." She reached up and kissed him softly.

"Mmmm. I could do no less. Now come back here and kiss me again." Several minutes passed while they were too agreeably engaged for conversation. Eventually, they fell asleep, cuddled together as they normally did.

As was usual since the shooting, the pair had not been asleep long when one began to thrash around. Both had been suffering nightmares for weeks, reliving the moments before, and in Darcy's case after, the event. It was not uncommon for the cries and movements of one to awaken the other early in the night, only for the situation to be reversed later. They always comforted each other, but the lack of sleep wore on them. As was the nature of each, they hid it well, and no one suspected anything was amiss at first.

On this particular night, it was Elizabeth whose screams first

Decisions and Consequences

woke the couple. She had the same dream every night—Wickham was pointing a gun at Darcy and fired. In this dream, he was struck in the arm just like he was during the incident. However, in the dream, his arm was always torn away and blood sprayed the inside of the carriage, causing her husband to die. She ended every dream on her knees beside him, holding him, and begging him not to leave her. Those screams were what always woke Darcy, and this night was no exception. He jolted awake, sitting straight up. He dragged her up with him and held her close, calling her name repeatedly and reassuring her of his life and good health. As always, when she awoke she was sobbing uncontrollably. Still he held her, rubbing her back and whispering endearments to her.

When they were finally able to go back to sleep, it was Darcy's turn to have a nightmare. His was similar to his wife's, except in his dream, Elizabeth died in his arms after being shot in the chest by Wickham. Elizabeth, who was unable to lift her husband due to her own injury and his size in comparison to hers, held him tightly and spoke in his ear, telling him of her love for him and assuring him she was well. They cried together until they exhausted themselves and fell back to sleep.

Soon, the lack of a full night's sleep began to take a toll on both of them. They began to have dark circles under their eyes. They grew short tempered with servants and family alike. They began to make mistakes in the accounts, Elizabeth in the household ones and Darcy in his estate accounts. Often, when these mistakes were pointed out to them, they could not comprehend how to make them right. Mrs. Bishop and Mr. Baxter noticed these things first, but felt their hands were tied. There was only so much

Decisions and Consequences

they could do as servants, despite being in service to the family for many years and feeling protective of them. They began dropping hints to Georgiana and Mary, hoping one of them would take a hint.

The first time one of the servants implied that her brother and sister were having difficulties, Georgiana brushed it off. She assumed they would ask for help if they needed it. Mary was not so sure and began observing her sister more closely. The second time, Georgiana, with Mary's blessing and assistance, decided to investigate and found Elizabeth at the edge of tears trying to figure out a menu. Though her new sister put on a pleasant expression, Georgiana could see the blackness around her eyes. She discussed it with Mary, and they decided to wait to speak. They would ask Fitzwilliam about it.

Her brother, however, denied there was anything wrong with

330

himself or his wife. He insisted they were fine and denied every suggestion that was made. In desperation, for by now she could see clearly what the housekeeper and butler had tried to tell them, Georgiana flew up the stairs to her room to pen an urgent missive to Colonel Fitzwilliam. She knew that her cousin and her brother were close, relying on each other to be honest in times of trouble. Finishing her note, she sanded it and sealed it and sent it off with a footman to the barracks where Richard was training his men.

Within an hour of receiving the message, the colonel was knocking on the door of Darcy House. He had decided on the way over to sit back and observe rather than jump into the fray with both feet. Arriving just before dinner, it did not take long for evidence of Georgiana's concerns to manifest itself. He watched silently as both Darcy and Elizabeth struggled to stay awake and respond coherently to the conversation. When the meal was over, he insisted on speaking to Darcy alone.

It took a further fifteen minutes to break down Darcy's defenses and discover that both he and his wife were suffering frequent nightmares. As a veteran of more battles than he cared to count, Richard could relate to what his cousins were dealing with.

"I am sorry for both of you. I have personal experience with nightmares, as I am sure you could guess."

Darcy nodded. "Yes, I should imagine so. I cannot fathom the horrors you have faced. How do you manage them? The nightmares, I mean."

"I am told there are many ways. At least, the older veterans advise me so. All are similar, but what works for me is to imagine the scenes in a different way. So for me, that would be bullets and sabers missing their targets and instead hitting trees or earth. Sometimes I simply force myself to look away, to the blue sky or to a field of flowers."

"And does this work? How can you force your dreams to change?"

"Yes, I am successful with this method. Have you never changed the paths in which your dreams travelled? Perhaps before this incident when you dreamed of your wife?"

Darcy blushed. He had, indeed, turned the direction of his dreams, often in tantalizing directions. He cleared his throat. His reprobate cousin did not need to know about the dreams he had of his beautiful and highly desirable wife. "Perhaps I will try this. Certainly it is a better idea than taking laudanum every night, which is the only other thing I knew to do."

Richard nodded, clapping his hand on his cousin's shoulder. "If it does not work, you will try the laudanum for a few days? Truly, Darcy, you look like death warmed over. Georgiana and Miss Mary are both concerned about you, and if the looks on the faces of the servants are any indication, they are as well. You must get some sleep, and so must Elizabeth if she is not to suffer a relapse."

Sighing heavily, Darcy admitted he was correct. "We cannot leave my sisters on their own while we sleep for days."

"Why do I not see if they would like to stay with my parents for a few days? You know they would love to have both girls. Georgiana was intended, by my mother, to stay for a few more weeks when Wickham attacked you, and chose instead to return here to help care for you. Surely she would not mind leaving you for another fortnight or so? I know for a fact she was not able to complete all the shopping she and my mother had planned. Miss Mary may not be as willing to leave, or she may prefer to visit her aunt and uncle instead of my parents. She has been quite devoted to the care of you and your wife. It is quite impressive." He paused. "I shall ask them when we return to the music room. If Georgiana agrees, she can return to Matlock House with me tonight. Or, she can wait until morning. I would guess Mother will hasten over to retrieve her. And Miss Mary will have time to make her decision, as well." He shook his head. "It is too bad my parents did not have more girl children. Mother is ever-eager to dress and coddle a daughter, and neither the Viscount nor I am anywhere close to offering for a lady and settling down."

Darcy snorted. "I fail to see why. Neither of you is getting any younger; it is not as though young ladies are not falling over your feet

Decisions and Consequences

at every ball and dinner you attend.
Then there is Miss Mary. I see you
watching her, and you never fail to
bring her name up in conversation."

"Come now, Darcy, you are
obviously tired; you have forgotten
to mind your tongue. Let us go join
our ladies."

Darcy rolled his eyes behind
his cousin, but followed him to the
music room. He sat beside his
wife, stretching his arm over the
back of the settee behind her.
When she leaned against him with
company in the house, he knew
she was tired. He wrapped his
arms around her and lay his head
on hers. He sighed, closing his
eyes. Richard, seeing the exhaustion in their faces, took it upon
himself to address the issue.

"Georgiana, Miss Mary, come
away from the pianoforte and talk
with us."

Surprised, they immediately
rose, gracefully walking across the

room, Georgiana to sit in a chair beside her brother and Mary on a settee across from her. Georgiana looked expectantly at her cousin, who stood a few feet away, back straight, hands clasped behind his back.

"I know that you are both aware of your brother and sister's behavior lately."

"I have. They are tired, and I know they are making mistakes they would not normally make," Georgiana replied.

Richard nodded. "Indeed. What you probably do not know is that they are suffering the effects of a lack of sleep." He softened his voice. "They are having nightmares about the shooting. Multiple nightmares, every night."

Georgiana's hand came up to her mouth. "Oh, Fitzwilliam, Elizabeth, I am so sorry! I feel terrible now that it took me so long to even notice something was wrong. Is there anything that can be done to help you?"

Mary, equally aghast, echoed the sentiment.

"Richard has suggested that we try to turn our minds away during the dreams. To imagine the events happening differently. He says it has helped him, so I plan to try it. One of us," Darcy indicated Elizabeth, "must get rest every night. If I can stop or lessen mine, I can better help Elizabeth with hers."

"Oh, how I long for a night of uninterrupted sleep," Elizabeth groaned. Darcy hugged her tighter.

"I know, my love. It will happen, I promise you."

Richard took up the conversation once more. "Georgiana, your brother is concerned with leaving you with just your companion while he and Elizabeth take a few days to sleep and recover. I recalled that you and Mother were not able to finish your shopping. I am certain she would love to have you back for a fortnight or so. What do you say? Miss Mary, she told me she would love to host you, as well. Or, if you prefer, you could stay with the Gardiners. I am certain they would welcome you."

Both girls nodded, seeing the sense in letting Fitzwilliam and Elizabeth have the house to themselves for a while. Georgiana spoke first. "I should like to do that, Richard. Fitzwilliam, are you certain you and Elizabeth will not need us?"

Darcy smiled. His baby sister had matured a great deal, a large part of it in the weeks since Wickham's attack, when she had helped care for them. "I am certain. Mrs. Bishop, Mr. Baxter, and our personal servants will see to us. We shall spend a great deal of time in sleep. We will be well on our own, but thank you. I am proud of the lady you have become, and I know Mama and Papa would be too, were they here to see you."

Georgiana's eyes filled with tears at the high praise from her brother. "Thank you," she whispered. Turning to her cousin, she stated, "I have some gowns still at Matlock House. Let me go up and alert my maid and Mrs. Annesley. I believe we can be ready to leave in a quarter of an hour."

Mary stood when Georgiana did. "I think I would like to go with Georgiana, if you are certain it is not an imposition."

"Not at all, Miss Mary! Mother was rather insistent that I attempt to persuade you."

"Very well, then. I will join Georgiana in preparing to leave."

Richard smiled. "Very good. I will wait here."

The girls took turns kissing Darcy and Elizabeth, hugging them tightly and wishing them a good rest, then headed up the staircase to their rooms. By the time they came back down, their brother and sister had been persuaded to go to theirs. The group of them, Richard, Georgiana, Mary, Mrs. Annesley, and Georgiana's maid, Amelia, boarded Darcy's carriage for the brief ride to Matlock House. Mary did not have a permanent maid of her own, so Lady Matlock would provide one, which was a good thing given how crowded the carriage was already.

Darcy and Elizabeth were asleep the moment their heads hit the pillows that night. This time, when the nightmares began, each of them did their best to turn the eyes of their mind away from the thing that frightened them. While they still had the nightmares that night, they felt as though they had not been as violent and heart-wrenching. Over the course of the next two weeks, by sleeping as much as they could and consistently applying Richard's advice, they began to recover from their exhaustion. It would take months for the nightmares to disappear completely, but they gradually became less horrifying. It was with great relief and warm greetings that the couple welcomed their sisters back home at the end of their fortnight with the Matlocks.

Chapter 14

Upon their return to Darcy House, both girls hugged Elizabeth as tightly as they dared. Elizabeth was happy to hug them in return, and held them close for a long time. Soon, though, she pulled back and wiped her sisters' tears.

"I am well, I promise, as is Fitzwilliam."

The girls moved to hug him, as well, a gesture he eagerly returned. He did not want either of them to worry over him.

"You certainly look well," Georgiana observed, running a critical eye over her brother's form. "Both of you have filled out a bit from the last time I saw you, and your eyes are bright again. Do you not agree, Mary?"

Decisions and Consequences

"I do! You look so much better than you did. I was so worried about you. Every day I asked for updates from Colonel Fitzwilliam and Lord and Lady Matlock."

Darcy smiled. "Yes, my valet told me of their visits. We are blessed to have family that cares so much." Realizing they were all still standing in the entrance hall, he urged the girls upstairs to refresh themselves, asking them to join him and Elizabeth in the library for tea in an hour.

Later that evening, after enjoying a day as a family, the Darcys and Mary met in the dining room for a meal. The group had barely started eating when the butler entered the room, bringing an unexpected guest.

"Richard!" Darcy exclaimed as he rose from his seat. "How are you? What brings you around at this time of the day?"

"Darcy, ladies." He bowed to each of them before he answered his cousin's question. "I am just come back from an errand for my general. I see you are sitting down to eat?"

"Yes, we are. Will you not join us?" Darcy asked. He could see that Mr. Baxter had anticipated this, knowing how close the two men were, and was already setting out a place for the colonel.

"Thank you, I believe I will. You know I would never turn down an opportunity to sample your cook's fare."

Darcy rolled his eyes as he returned to his seat. Soon, conversation was flowing.

The good colonel was happy to see Miss Mary at the table. He had found her intriguing in Hertfordshire, and after spending time with her at Matlock House, he found that his feelings for her were growing deeper. After the meal, the male members of the party remained in the dining room to enjoy a glass of port while the ladies retired to the music room.   Richard wasted no time asking Darcy about Miss Mary.

"She is Miss Bennet now, you know.   While Elizabeth and I were recovering from our wounds, the eldest married Bingley."

"Did she? I remember his proposal at your engagement ball. Brave lad, he was.   Even were I certain that my suit was welcome, I am not sure I would be willing to ask that question in front of the entire neighborhood!"

Darcy laughed.   "Yes, he was rather brave, was he not?" Pulling himself from those memories, he addressed his cousin.   "What do you want to know about Mary?"

"I noticed her in Hertfordshire; she was...interesting."

"Preachy."

"Well, yes," Richard chuckled, "but I saw that when she received attention, she lost her somberness. She almost glowed when you and my father danced with her.   I saw

346

the same thing tonight at dinner. You know, she is every bit as beautiful as your Elizabeth."

Darcy scowled, growling, "Do not forget she *is **my*** Elizabeth." He did not like anyone else noticing his wife's good qualities.

"Easy now," Richard responded uneasily. "I meant no disrespect. You must admit, she is beautiful. I am certain many men admire her. Surely you are proud of that."

Darcy gave him a hard glare for several moments before finally letting go of his affront. "I apologize. Since I came to the realization that I love my wife, I find myself almost irrationally jealous at the mere thought of another man looking at her." He paused and ran his hand through his hair. "I know not what I shall do when we begin attending balls and dinners, and they must be allowed to touch her."

Richard shook his head, not quite understanding his cousin's position. "Look at it this way, Darcy, no one will be able to cite ugliness as a reason for disliking her. Anyone who sees you together must admit, you are well-matched, physically. Both of you are handsome."

Darcy snorted inelegantly. "That we are. She is the perfect complement to me in every way. The best decision I ever made was to offer for her." Suddenly realizing he had become distracted, he brought the conversation back around to Mary. "Why do you ask such questions about my sister?"

Relieved that Darcy had backed away from his unreasonable, jealous anger, the colonel was hesitant to make the situation worse. However, he had brought it up and now he must follow through. "I should like to get to know her better. I wanted to inform you of my interest in her."

"What outcome are you hoping to see?"

Richard did not answer right away. Licking his lips, he looked down at the glass of wine in his hand and considered what to say. After a few minutes, during which Darcy remained totally silent, Richard began. "As you know, I am near to thirty years of age. I have worked hard to gain my rank. I do not make much, but Father gives me an allowance, as do you."

Darcy nodded, waiting patiently for Richard to continue, "You know that I have saved as much as I could. You have helped me with it, pointing me to sound investments. I have saved enough that I feel I can now marry. I have had many opportunities to observe Miss Mary ...excuse me, Miss Bennet... both here as she cared for you and your wife and at Matlock House. Her loving care for those around her is refreshing. She is not unintelligent, and I know that my mother urged her to read more than sermons while she was with them. She has a quick mind. I believe she would make an excellent mate." He paused, considering how much he should reveal, and finally decided to be circumspect. "I am impressed with her, and that is all I will say. I plan to continue to observe her during the season, to talk with her and dance with her, perhaps call on her. Should she prove to be the young lady I believe she is and should she remain unattached at the end of the season, I plan to offer for her."

"And if she falls in love with someone else?"

Richard sighed. "Then I shall have to start my search over."

"Your heart is not engaged?"

"Not yet." Richard gave his cousin a small smile and then looked down again. "But it could be. I am attracted to her, but I have seen far more than any man should have to. I have seen war, and I am scarred inside, where it cannot be seen. I am not worthy of any gently bred woman, not really. So, if she should find happiness with another, I would gladly let her go. I do hope, however, that the attraction becomes a mutual one."

He looked up to see Darcy watching him speculatively. He remained quiet, knowing from experience his cousin saw something in him that he perhaps did not want to be seen.

"I suspect your heart is already engaged, Richard. If it were not, you would not be willing to let her go and look further."

Richard felt Darcy's words arrow deep into his heart.

"Do you wish me to say anything to Mary? It goes without saying, I will tell her sister. Elizabeth would be greatly displeased if I kept that sort of information to myself."

"I understand you must tell your wife; I would rather Mary not know anything just yet, though.

Decisions and Consequences

Give me time to get to know her better and be sure of my own mind. I will warn you before I make any move to court her."

Darcy nodded. "Very well. I trust you with my life, and I am satisfied you will behave honorably. Now," he said, pushing himself up from his chair with his hands on the table, "let us go rejoin the ladies. I find myself becoming anxious when I am too long parted from my Elizabeth."

They strolled to the music room, enjoying the sound of the pianoforte and trying to guess who was playing. They peeked around the edge of the door and upon discovering it was Mary playing, Darcy shook his head, digging into his pocket for a five-pound note then slapping it into Richard's hand. His cousin laughed, clapping him on the shoulder before sauntering into the room.

"What was that all about?" Elizabeth had seen the performance at the door and rolled her eyes at her husband's petulant expression.

"Just a small wager between cousins. Never fear, I left him plenty with which to pay the bills."

"Thank you for that," was her dry response. She wrapped her arms around her husband as he pulled her into his embrace. "Are you pouting, my darling?"

"I am a Darcy," he sniffed. "Darcys do not pout."

Her eyebrow rose. "Oh, I believe they do. You just did."

Changing the subject, her husband looked to the pianoforte, where Mary sat with her mouth agape. She had stopped playing when she saw her new brother embrace her sister. Georgiana, who sat next her and had been turning pages, elbowed her in the side, startling her into closing her mouth.

"You must become used to such things, Mary," she whispered. "You know that ever since they were injured, they have been more and more affectionate with each other. They do not do so outside of our home, but here is another matter. If they become too lost in each other, we shall simply take ourselves elsewhere and shut the door behind us. Also," Georgiana added, almost as an afterthought, "I think we must never enter a room with a closed door unless we knock first. They often do not think to lock it behind them." She gave her new sister a significant look.

Mary blushed. "Yes, you are correct. I should be inured to their displays by now, should I not be?"

"Please, do not think badly of them. They are in love. I am so happy for Fitzwilliam. He deserves everything good, and Mrs. Annesley has explained to me that when two people are married and in love, they often forget themselves. I would put up with much worse to see my brother smile so, I can assure you."

Mary nodded; Georgiana's words made sense. "I feel the same about Elizabeth. But, Georgiana...are we not taught that it is wrong to behave so? To hug and kiss a man?"

"Mrs. Annesley says that for a maiden and a single man it is wrong, but for a married couple, nothing that happens between them is, as long as both consent. She did not give me details, as she says I am too young to know of such things, but she said there are many ways for a couple to show their love." Georgiana sighed. "Sometimes I wish I were older. So much is not explained and I am left to imagine. Sometimes I am fearful of what the future will bring. Do you not agree?"

Before Mary could answer, Richard interrupted them. "Please Miss Bennet, continue your playing. I was greatly enjoying it when I entered the room. You play delightfully."

Mary blushed. "As long as Georgiana does not mind, I should be glad to."

Georgiana replied that she was perfectly content to listen to Mary and continue to turn pages for her. They spent the next hour taking turns playing before their fingers grew tired and they stopped. The group spent a few minutes longer talking amongst themselves but soon decided to retire for the night. Being a frequent guest as well as a member of the family, the staff kept a room at the ready for Richard, so he spent the night at Darcy House.

That night, in the afterglow of their loving, Darcy brought up his discussion with Fitzwilliam. Elizabeth was thrilled that her most invisible sister had caught the eye of such an eligible gentleman. Understanding her new cousin's reasoning, she agreed to keep the information from Mary, at least for the time being.

Elizabeth knew from the way her husband held himself that there was more on his mind than just her sister and his cousin. Wanting to get whatever it was out in the open before they fell asleep, she asked him about it.

"What is wrong? You have something on your mind. I see the signs in your behavior."

Darcy sighed. "I have something to tell you but I am hesitant. I know I should and I will have to, but..." He paused, gathering his thoughts. "I am afraid of losing your good opinion once again, but after my talk with Richard, I feel that it is not right to keep it from you."

"Goodness, it sounds serious! Please, Fitzwilliam, tell me. Having a strong marriage is too important to me to allow something to fester in one of us that has the potential to come between us."

"I agree that we need to talk about the things that bother us." He

Decisions and Consequences

sighed again, deeply, before plunging into his tale. "Do you remember when we were in Longbourn's parlor after you had spoken to your father and chosen me to marry?"

"Yes, I do."

"Do you recall asking me about the information I possess that I shared with him? And how I refused to speak of it because he had not?"

"I do." By now, Elizabeth was staring at him, certain she was about to receive the answer to her long-ago request for information.

"Your father, well, your grandfather's will contained certain requirements for Mr. Bennet's wife if he were to receive the estate as his. If he did not marry within those specifications, Longbourn was to go to Mr. Colllins' father and then to Mr. Collins himself, eventually. I tried to use that information to convince your father to make you marry me." By the time he was finished speaking,

Darcy could not look Elizabeth in the face. Instead, he played with a long tendril of her hair, focusing his gaze on that to avoid seeing the anger and disdain he was sure would be in her eyes. When she did not speak after several minutes, he was forced to look up.

Elizabeth was staring over his shoulder, deep in contemplation. Her first response was anger, but then she recalled her father's decision to let her choose. He did not force her to choose one over the other. She could have married her cousin and hoped for the best. True, she was happy now, but it had taken time and work, weeks and months of work, to see her chosen husband's good qualities. She knew he loved her, and the fact that he would share this now and endanger that happiness spoke volumes of his character.

"Elizabeth?"

Looking into his eyes, she responded. "Do not think I am happy to hear this news. I am not. I am displeased with you for using it as you did, but I know that you promised to keep silent on the matter. You have proven yourself an honorable man, though a little arrogant at times, and a good and faithful husband. I know that you will keep that promise."

"Thank you," he whispered, leaning in to softly kiss her lips. "I love you. I did not when I used that information, at least, I did not think I did. I wanted you, though. I knew you were perfect for Pemberley, and I think deep down I knew you were perfect for me. I am so sorry I stooped to such levels."

"I forgive you. To be honest, I am equally upset with my father for putting his family in such a precarious situation. How did Mr. Collins not know this?"

After a long discussion of the particulars and an examination into what could have happened, Elizabeth kissed him. "Thank you for telling me. You did not have to. I doubt I would have ever known. Even though I am upset and a little angry about it, I can see that by sharing this with me, you have shown me great respect, and I appreciate that. Knowing that I do have that from you makes it easier to forgive you, and it makes me love you all the more."

"Thank you, my love. I will never keep anything from you again. Well, I shall try not to; if it is in my power to tell you, I will. I love you too much to risk your ire." He kissed her tenderly, holding her close, and soon they fell into a deep slumber, wrapped in each other's arms.

~~~***~~~

The very next night the Darcy party attended the first ball of the season. Elizabeth's wound was healed, though it remained tender to the touch and she used a sling when at home. She arranged a shawl over her shoulders to hide the still ugly scar. With time, it would fade to white and not be quite so noticeable but for now, it needed to remain out of sight. They took Mary with them, and she was beautiful in a white evening gown with green trim.

As they were announced at Lord and Lady Stewart's ball, those in attendance fell silent. Everyone had heard of the attack, and a few had been in the vicinity at the time it happened and had seen Darcy carry his wife out of one carriage and into another. Rumors abounded, from speculation that the attacker was a vagrant to more salacious theories, such as a jealous lover of Elizabeth's. She was still so new to the *ton* that, despite the general feeling of approbation toward her, so little was known of her as to make it easy to lay the blame at her feet. The Matlocks had done their best to dispel the rumors, but not everyone had listened.

Idle reports of the reasons behind her injuries were not enough to cow Elizabeth, though, and Darcy followed her lead.

The pair of them, Mary in tow, made the rounds of the room, greeting first their hosts and then the rest. Mary was introduced to everyone, and as her connection to Darcy made her a lady of great interest, she soon found her dance card completely filled. To her great relief, one of those dances had been reserved by Colonel Fitzwilliam, who had arrived just after they did. He had asked for and been granted the supper set. One set was reserved for Darcy, and one each for Lord Matlock and Viscount Tansley, the colonel's older brother.

Though she had not known him long, Mary found she rather liked the colonel. He was always respectful of her, asking her opinion and listening carefully to her replies. He had a gentle way of making her question her conclusions that she preferred to her father's mocking responses. When she saw him enter the dining room at Darcy House the evening before, she was struck by the good humor in his face. He was not as handsome as her brother, but his ready smile made her forget that fact. Her heart had skipped a beat when he turned it on her and bowed to her in greeting. That had never happened before, and she was not sure what it meant. She had not the opportunity today to discuss it with Elizabeth, but she intended to on the morrow.

Mary danced every set that night and left the event exhausted. On the way home, Elizabeth asked about her night, and it was with enthusiasm that belied her tiredness that she assured her sister it was the best night she had ever had. Never in Meryton had Mary been asked to dance more than once or twice. It was a novel experience to be the center of attention. Given her serious nature, she wondered at it, but did not allow negative thoughts to rob her of the happiness the night had given her.

"And what of Colonel Fitzwilliam?"

"Oh, Lizzy, he is such a nice man," Mary earnestly responded. "He never speaks down to me or mocks me. I always feel as though what I say matters to him."

"Did anyone else you met tonight elicit that feeling?"

Mary thought for a moment before replying. "Not really. There were two or three who appeared to listen to every word I said, but none who caused me to feel that I could say anything and not be censured. Does that make sense?"

Elizabeth nodded in the dark, though her sister could not see her. "I think so. You felt as though the colonel gave credence to your opinions instead of disregarding them."

"Yes! That is it exactly!"

The carriage was coming to a stop at that moment outside their townhouse. Darcy added his two pence to the conversation before handing the ladies out. "My cousin was raised much as I was, to value women and see them as rational creatures capable of great thoughts. No lady who can efficiently run the household of a great estate, or even a small one, could be stupid. He will make a fine husband to whomever he offers his hand." With that, he handed the ladies out and their conversation came to an end.

For Elizabeth and Darcy, the ball was equally exhausting, though for different reasons. They did dance, and arranged it so that Elizabeth's first sets were all family. In like manner to her sister, she opened with her husband, then danced with the colonel, the viscount, and the earl. Her supper dance was reserved for Darcy, who had danced with Mary and the countess in addition to his wife. Their supper set completed the allowable number of dances for one couple, and so Darcy spent the meal alternately grumbling about only being allowed to dance twice with his own wife and listening to his cousin's conversation with Mary.

After supper, neither Darcy chose to dance. Instead, they alternately sat together amongst friends and acquaintances or strolled the edge of the room, seeing and being seen. Elizabeth's quick wit and teasing manner soon reminded all in attendance why they liked her. She left with many promises of calls and teas, and made a few of her own.

Darcy was proud of his wife, and he was beginning to see that the impertinence he despised when he first met her stood her in good stead with those who would disparage her. She was easily able to deflect criticism, often turning the critic's words back upon herself, and frequently without the person knowing what happened. He thoroughly enjoyed watching her decimate her opponents, and when they reached their rooms that night, he made his approbation abundantly clear.

~~~***~~~

The day following the ball, no one was surprised when the good colonel was the first gentleman to arrive to call on Mary. Being family to the Darcys, he felt it his right to remain all day and his cousin was enjoying the spectacle too much to bother asking him to leave. Richard glowered at every other gentleman who came to visit, though he did manage to refrain from lambasting them with his tongue.

Where Darcy was amused by the colonel's behavior, Mary was soothed by it. She had, if anything, understated her feelings about him to her sister and brother the previous night. She greatly admired the gentleman and appreciated his presence. She knew better than to let her feelings rule her actions, and wanted to enjoy more of the season and the attention it brought, but she also was aware that if, at any time, Colonel Fitzwilliam confessed to feelings for her, she would accept him.

For the remainder of the season, the Darcys continued to attend balls and routs, dinner parties and soirees, escorting their sister. The colonel always attended, and as the weeks passed, he began to attend to Mary more closely. It was not long before the other gentlemen stopped calling, for Richard was always there, planted by her side along with her family.

At the end of the season, Mary Bennet became Mrs. Richard Fitzwilliam. The colonel retired his commission soon after, and the happy couple moved into their newly-purchased estate, Briarwood,

Decisions and Consequences

which was a mere fifty miles of good road from Pemberley. When the Bingleys finally gave up Netherfield and purchased their own estate, Hanley Court, the three sisters were satisfied to be within half a day's drive of each other.

~~~***~~~

Mr. and Mrs. Bennet, once their children were grown, were all at sixes and sevens for a time. With no daughters to distract her, Mrs. Bennet was forever invading her husband's bookroom, to his great dismay. He began making frequent trips to Derbyshire to visit his three eldest daughters, while his wife began spending more time in London and Kent with her youngest children and their families. They spent very little time at home, but both were at Longbourn when Mrs. Bennet passed one cold winter night after a bout of pneumonia lasting several weeks. Mr. Bennet was with her to the end. His demeanor for the rest of his life was solemn and subdued. He also passed, about six months later, in his sleep. Those who knew him well speculated that, as much as he mocked and ridiculed his wife, he had loved her deeply and could not live without her, choosing to follow her in death.

Elizabeth and Darcy lived a happy fifty years together, raising five sons and four daughters. The estate prospered under their management, their wealth rising to heights his ancestors could have only hoped to reach. They saw each child happily married, and eagerly cuddled five and twenty grandchildren and ten great-grandchildren during their lifetimes. They passed away within a half hour of each other, still in the same bed they had shared their entire married life.

The End

Decisions and Consequences

About the Author

Zoe Burton first fell in love with Jane Austen's books in 2010, after seeing the 2005 version of Pride and Prejudice on television. While making her purchases of Miss Austen's novels, she discovered Jane Austen Fan Fiction; soon after that she discovered websites full of JAFF. Her life has never been the same. She began writing her own stories when she ran out of new ones to read.

Zoe lives in the snow-belt of Ohio. She is a Special Education Teacher in an online school, and has a passion for romance in general, Pride and Prejudice in particular, and NASCAR.

Zoe is a member of the Romance Writers of America, the Northeast Ohio chapter of the RWA, the Beau Monde chapter of the RWA, the Jane Austen Society of North America, and

JASNA's Ohio North Coast chapter.

Connect with Zoe Burton

Email:
zoeburtonauthor@outlook.com

Twitter:
@zoeburtonauthor

Facebook:
https://www.facebook.com/ZoeBurtonBooks

Blog:
austenpromises.wordpress.com